THE CELTIC WITCH AND THE SORCERER

The Celtic Witch and the Sorcerer

by

Lyn Armstrong

Resplendence Publishing, LLC
http://www.resplendencepublishing.com

Resplendence Publishing, LLC
P.O. Box 992
Edgewater, Florida, 32132

The Celtic Witch and the Sorcerer
Copyright © 2008, Lyn Armstrong
Edited by Tiffany Mason
Cover art by Rika Singh
Print format ISBN: 978-1934992036
Electronic format ISBN: 978-934992029

Warning: All rights reserved. The unauthorized reproduction or distribution of this copyrighted work is illegal. Criminal copyright infringement, including infringement without monetary gain, is investigated by the FBI and is punishable by up to 5 years in federal prison and a fine of $250,000.

Electronic release: January, 2008
Trade paperback printing: March, 2008

This is a work of fiction. Names, characters, places, and occurrences are a product of the author's imagination. Any resemblance to actual persons, living or dead, places, or occurrences, is purely coincidental.

LYN ARMSTRONG'S CELTIC SERIES

The Last Celtic Witch – Book One
Available now at www.resplendencepublishing.com and www.amazon.com.

Heart of a Warlock – Book Three
Available July 2008

Witch Hunter – Book Four
Available October 2008

DEDICATION

The Celtic Witch and the Sorcerer is dedicated to my real life hero and husband, Grant.
His love, support and devotion is purely magical. He *is* my sorcerer.

ACKNOWLEDGEMENTS

I would like to acknowledge these incredible writers/editors who have helped me over the years: Helen Rosburg whose mentoring helped guide me through the confusing waters of editing. Heather Graham for her generous spirit and showing me what it means to be humble in this crazy business. Traci Hall for always having my back and making me laugh. Kimberly Gonzalez for her untapped knowledge on history. Aleka Nakis, the promotional guru and all round cheerleader. And for Tiffany Mason, my editor and friend, who has talked me off the window ledge time and again.

These ladies are truly inspirational and are a huge part of my writing success.
They are my creative sisters.

CHAPTER ONE

Lady Gavenia could not believe her eyes. From the corner where her spirit floated, she stared down at the bed where her cold, lifeless body laid, still covered in blood from birthing her new born babe.

"Milady is dead!" the midwife sobbed, placing her hand on the shoulder of Gavenia's mother.

No amount of comfort or words seemed to move Lady Adela MacAye. Her round face drained of all color as if her heart were stolen from her chest. Tears streamed down her cheeks, even though her normally warm brown eyes were frozen to the depths.

"She can't be dead."

The midwife shook her head. "I am afraid the birth of the child was too much to bear."

Her mother pushed the midwife to the side and threw her arms around Gavenia's shoulders, rocking the lifeless body back and forth, chanting, "I am so sorry, I am so sorry." Her words were filled with an emotion Gavenia never wanted to hear, the grief of a parent who watched their child die.

Her mother lovingly touched her ashen face, yet Gavenia felt nothing. No caress, no warmth. Anger burned deep inside her, hurt brewed like a wicked potion. No one should have to experience this. What had she done to deserve this vision?

The answer came as the oak door crashed open, silhouetting a man she had never seen before. His body shook with rage as he stepped into the chamber. The ladies huddled closer.

Who was he?

For certain, he did not come from Gleich Castle. His tall stature would stand out among the village folk. Although she could not discern his shadowed face beneath the hood, his eyes glowed with an unholy light.

"She is dead." He drew his sword from the scabbard, the scraping of metal echoed off the castle walls.

Her mother's emotions suddenly surged through the room, and she ran at the stranger. But before she could reach him, his words stopped her.

"And you killed her."

* * * * *

Gavenia opened her eyes, her heart pounding with anxiety. She wiped the perspiration from her forehead and breathed deep of the night, trying to calm herself.

Another death vision.

The muscles in her back ached. She raised her arms above her head and moaned while stretching to relieve the tensed knot. Foreseeing her death was not a power she wished to have, but as a Celtic witch, one did not get a choice.

She rose from the sable-lined chair. The stone runes seemed heavier in her hands as Gavenia returned them to a drawstring velvet pouch and absently dropped the bag onto the table. Sighing, she collapsed onto the bed. Her cream-colored gown made from the finest cloth billowed around her ankles as she lifted her legs and hugged them to her chest.

Ever since her third winter, Gavenia was burdened with the same vision. Being the last line of Celtic witches, her family demanded she produce a child to inherit her powers of good magick. She was as duty bound as a revered cow procreating in the pasture.

Her mother would say that one day, the *chosen one* would come into her life—the one man who could sire a babe to carry her ancestral powers.

Gavenia would smile at her mother and change the subject. Her mother was unaware of the death vision and that Gavenia would risk death if she lay with a man. To Gavenia, men were dangerous and she went to great perils to stay well away from them.

After all, a life alone was preferable to no life at all.

Gavenia lifted her thick hair above her neck, allowing the cool mountain breeze from the large arch window to caress her warm skin.

A light knock sounded on her door.

"Come," she answered, rising to her feet.

Her older brother, Sir Callum, entered and absently sat upon her bed, wrinkling her yellow kirtle. "I bested Father in chess last eve. You should have seen his face." His dimples deepened. "The mighty chieftain beaten by his son."

Gavenia stared at her brother of twenty-two winters. Like her, he was the water reflection of their father. His angelic features, long blond hair and structured jaw line stole many maidens' hearts. But what endeared Callum to all was his carefree nature. Bestowed knighthood at a young age, the future chieftain of the Roberts clan was the first born of a Celtic witch and Highland laird. Callum's charm was irresistible, making it hard for Gavenia to stay angry when he teased her as a child.

She tugged at the garment beneath her brother. "Get off."

He shuffled to the side and she snatched her kirtle from under him, replacing it in a long jeweled chest at the foot of her bed.

"You are in a foul disposition this morn. Did you have another death vision?"

"Why do you ask?" she snapped.

"You are always sullen afterwards."

"You would be too if you saw yer death over and over again."

"Why not tell me of this vision?"

"Nae."

"I would do all within my power to see you are kept safe. Even protect you with a thousand soldiers."

Gavenia smiled. "I wish not to burden those I love with this knowledge. And besides, some things not even you can protect me from."

"Mother's death vision did not come true—perhaps the same will be for you."

"Mother did not see herself die, merely the events leading to her death. I have seen my corpse."

Callum rose and pulled her into his arms. "I am sorry that yer powers are a curse as well as a blessing."

Gavenia pushed him away. "I choose not to think of it."

"You are right. Let us rejoice in the moment. It is all we have." He sauntered to the door. "Prepare yourself. Mother seeks an audience with you. She has news of my betrothal and yearns to throw a feast in celebration of the alliance." His voice rose in a melodious tone, "and no doubt she hopes to snare… you… a… husband."

Gavenia groaned and turned her back on her brother. His laughter muffled by the door closing behind him.

She would have to dissuade her mother. Thus far, she had reached twenty winters without an arrangement, but the time would soon come when she must accept a man's betrothal.

'Twas not fair.

Her life was spent behind the protective walls of Gleich Castle. Her family denied her every occasion to explore the world, saying it was unsafe for a witch in these times. Only the Roberts clan accepted the Celtic witches as good instead of evil. Outside, people were superstitious. Their ignorant fear had caused her grandmother's death.

Trapped by protection and duty. That was her boring life until she died.

Assailed by a terrible sense of bitterness, she picked up the comb and yanked it through her hair. "I will never marry or touch a mon. Never!"

* * * * *

"Mother, I am not interested in men. I would rather travel to Paris or Rome and meet new people."

"Are you trying to hurt me?" her mother asked, hands firmly placed on her slender hips.

Adela MacAye Roberts was a woman of serene beauty. With brown hair and deep soulful eyes, she was gifted with grace and compassion. Except when it came to Gavenia finding her *chosen one*.

"Daughter, you have an easy life of acceptance. Do you realize how hard it can be outside the safety of Gleich Castle?"

Gavenia rolled her eyes. "Aye, Mother. I know you had a trying life as a Celtic Witch."

"*Trying* would not cover the constant terror of being discovered and then burned like yer grandmother."

"Our family history is full of tragedy, but that does not mean I must be forced into choosing a husband and spending my life behind these walls."

"Not just any husband, he must be the *chosen one*."

"A mon with a pure heart who calls to you... I know the proverb, Mother."

"Only he will have the bloodline to breed healthy girls that can wield our ancient powers." Adela shifted a stray hair from Gavenia's face, and her voice softened. "I canna cast the spell, only you can."

Gavenia stepped away from her mother and averted her eyes. "I will not, Mother. Can you not accept that I do not like men?"

"You need not be afraid of them, my dear. The chosen one will not harm you."

Shaking her head, Gavenia groaned, "I do not want a husband. Why can Callum not be the one to pass on the powers? No doubt his betrothed will be a strong lass, surely their heirs would produce another Celtic witch."

"I love yer brother, but I canna rely on his blood to sustain our powers. You know he has yet to show any signs of Celtic influence. The true magick resides in women, and each generation holds an extra gift." Her mother's eyes watered. "If I could have had more babies survive, then I wouldn't need to burden you… but alas…"

Gavenia turned and snaked her arm in the crook of her mother's elbow.

"'Tis not yer fault, Mother. The fates have chosen for you to only have two children."

Adela smiled through moist eyes. "And I bless Arianrhod Goddess every day for you both." She touched Gavenia's cheek. "Perchance, I might still have another baby. Yer father and I do not lack for encouragement."

"Oh, Mother!" Gavenia pushed away.

The tinkle of her mother's laugh washed over Gavenia and she smiled in return. In these moments, she saw her mother still held the presence of youth.

"One day you will find a mon that will make yer blood heat with a mere glance and when you do, yer life will be charged with a magick that goes beyond yer powers."

"I do not think that will happen."

A mischievous glint shone in Adela's eyes. She grasped both Gavenia's hands and took a deep breath. Closing her eyelids, she chanted beneath her breath.

"Mother, what are you doing?"

She continued to chant.

Gavenia squirmed; she did not want to conjure the chosen one. She was not ready to die.

"Mother, you need not do this."

"Shh." Adela chanted again and then stopped, the air crackled with energy as a blue, round light floated down from the rafters in between the two women.

"Show me a sign of who will win my daughter's heart."

"Mother!"

The orb stretched into a shield of the Robert's clan. The honorable wolf glowed bright and strong.

Gavenia said, "You see? 'Tis of our clan. This is a sign I will not marry."

The image changed and Gavenia felt her heart beat increase. A black shadow snaked around the shield, transforming the noble crest to a demonic boar. Malevolent eyes glowed while sharp teeth dripped with dark red blood. The shadow exploded, forcing the witches apart.

Fear gripped Gavenia, twisting her insides. She glanced at her mother, whose panicked face reflected her own.

Adela crawled over and gathered Gavenia into her arms. "I will not let anything hurt you."

"Dark forces surround the chosen one. How could I summon him now when he would bring death to our clan?"

"We do not know for sure that was the meaning."

Gavenia pulled away from the warm embrace. "Do not presume innocence. You and I both felt the power of evil."

"Perhaps the chosen one needs help."

"I would not help a stranger if it meant the clan's peril."

"The chosen one is no stranger, he is yer family. The one destined to bring you love and happiness."

"I will not do it."

"You must summon him. You must beget an heir at any cost. The future of good magick is at stake."

Tears wet Gavenia's face. Unable to hold the raw emotion inside, she cried, "Please, I canna."

Running out the door, she ignored her mother's concerned voice as Adela called after her.

* * * * *

"Tell me...who do you serve?" Tremayne asked as he slammed the heavy door.

His voluptuous sex maid jumped from the noise. Wringing her hands, she walked further into his chamber, no doubt to put distance between his anger and herself. Coira MacKinnon might be a scheming, lying whore, but she knew when to retreat.

She pivoted toward him—her auburn hair tumbling around her shoulders as her hazel eyes lowered. "Ye are Laird Tremayne Campbell, chieftain of the clan, son to Lady Torella, and the great dark sorcerer of this castle."

"I am glad you remembered, Coira." Tremayne went to his timber chest beneath the tall window and opened the lid. Without looking at her, he continued, "Explain why you disobeyed my command?"

"Master, I wish not to leave you," she pleaded and ran to his side. She went to place her hand on his shoulder, but in the last moment, withdrew. "I pray you; send one of the old crones in my stead."

He straightened and pulled out a long whip. "Mayhaps, yer loyalties need to be prompted as to who is yer laird."

Coira blinked, her lips curving into a smile at the sight of the whip in his hand. "How may I assist you?" She began to unlace her ruby corset and threw it to the side, eagerness shining in her eyes.

"I know you like the whip, Coira. But this time I will *not* use it on you until you plead for forgiveness."

"Please do not tease me, Master." She lifted a linen chemise over her head, her pert breasts jutting proudly, the peaks hard and erect.

Tremayne felt his member rise, throbbing beneath his kilt. His hands cupped her breasts and she groaned. Curly, copper hair cascaded over soft shoulders while Coira arched her back, pushing her chest forward.

"I would do anything for you my laird. I beg you to forgive my impertinence."

Taller than the average man, Tremayne looked down his nose at the contrite maid. "You will offer yer services to Lady Gavenia of the Roberts clan."

Coira raised her head and scrunched her nose. "I could be of more use to you in yer bedchamber, my laird. Do not punish me by sending me away."

Tremayne chuckled nastily, and distanced himself from her, releasing the sexual energy he wrapped around his lovers.

Eerie, cool air surrounded Coira. Smiling, he watched the bumps rise on her delicate skin. His touch inspired submission, but taking it away would send a woman into a state of uncontrollable wanting, leaving them consumed by a deadly thirst for something only he could provide.

Turning, he looped the whip around his neck and walked over to the wooden table to pour a chalice of red wine. "I grow weary of yer whining." Taking a sip of the tart liquid, he studied Coira's curves. Her body had given him much pleasure and her sexual energy fed his powers, yet he grew restless for something. He knew not what. "Perhaps it is time to send you back to yer father. I know he could use yer help in the fields."

"Nae, my laird."

She ran toward him and then halted. Coira knew not to touch him without being instructed to do so. Backing away, she lowered her head, falling to her knees before him. "I am ready to be punished."

The light surrounding Coira's aura was dark red, impatient to feel the sting of the whip. Some women liked to be caressed with a tender hand while others, like Coira, were stimulated by power and violence. No matter the method, Tremayne absorbed their energy when they reached their sexual peak.

Replacing the goblet, he slowly pulled the whip from his shoulders and cracked the leather bind near her feet. The sharp sound made her body jolt, and the energy surrounding her increased with sexual tension.

"You will report to me on everything Lady Roberts does."

Coira nodded, her eyes glazed with lust and submission. Grabbing the back of her neck, he pulled her up and threw her across the bed, face down, her bare backside exposed to him.

With a flick of his wrist the whip lightly snaked across her flesh and she groaned.

"Who her companions are."

The whip cracked in the air.

"Where she rides."

This time, the thin leather cut lightly into her flesh.

"Oh," she moaned. "Aye, it will be done. Please, punish me again."

Tremayne smiled, the scent of her arousal reached him and he breathed with satisfaction. There was nothing more intoxicating than a woman's nectar.

He ran the handle of the whip up the length of her inner thighs until he reached the apex. "Open yer legs," he commanded, his tone brooked no argument.

She complied and he rubbed the handle up and down her sleek, moist lips. Her muffled sounds came from the bedcovers, she wiggled against the whip.

His cock pulsed against the rough fabric of his kilt, but he ignored the constrained ache. Tilting the handle, he slowly eased it inside her. Backwards and forwards, he watched Coira's aura change from red to deep purple as her arousal increased. Soon, she would give him her life-force.

"Take my whip. Take it!"

"Aye," she screamed, her body enveloping the handle further.

She shrieked, her body shuddering with pleasure. Sizzling energy gathered around her like a glowing cloak. The purple light crackled as it filled Tremayne's body, creating a mystical sensation beyond any physical pleasure. He quickly pulled out the handle and kneeled behind her. Biting his lip with frustration, he lifted his kilt and drove into her warm, pulsating core.

Thoughts of the Celtic witch fueled his thrusts; harder and harder he pushed inside Coira, punishing his sex maid.

Soon, very soon, he would be in a position to spill the blood of Lady Gavenia Roberts.

CHAPTER TWO

Tremayne entered the drafty hall with little enthusiasm. Several of his hunting wolves scrabbled to his side, vying for his attention. He spared them a passing glance and gave the largest wolf a brisk pat. For some reason, animals were drawn to him. Perhaps they sensed that their affectionate touch was the only contact he allowed himself.

Stepping over a black pup, he tried to ignore the filthy hall. He sat on the high chair and surveyed the great chamber. The moldy rushes gave off an unpleasant odor while last eve's meal remained on the trestles. Intoxicated soldiers and rambunctious maids covered tables and benches, entwined with one another in carnal abandonment. Their lusty groans filled the air while a dark ruby light surrounded their bodies.

Tremayne breathed deeply.

Sexual energy from the clan infused his body and soul. He held out his hands, his long fingers shaking from the intense power coursing through his veins. Soon, very soon, his skin would settle and his heart beat would slow to its usual rhythm. It did not take long in the morn for his mortal body to adjust to his sorcerer's heritage.

The chair beside him scraped against the floor. Tremayne tilted his head to study the man who had looked after him since he was born. With a long nose and weak chin, Evan Campbell's brown eyes appeared more sunken then they really were. His lanky body and thin arms made him seem weak, yet one should not be fooled by appearances. Tremayne still held the childhood scars from when Evan whipped him for being too loud in his tower prison.

The elder man sat down with a hump and banged a tankard on the table. "Bring me ale, wench!" he barked at a passing servant.

Tremayne leaned casually back into the chair, his jaw muscle tensed.

"What vexes you this morn?" Evan asked, his attention on a busty brunette lifting her skirt to tease one of the guards. The overweight soldier fell to his knees and rubbed his face in her exposed black curly hair.

Tremayne pointed to the flies buzzing around the old meat in front of him. "I am vexed by the filth in this hall."

A loud groan came from a red-haired soldier, his backside rose and fell with each thrust into a plump, pretty maid. She was bending over a table, her yellow kirtle up around her waist.

Evan faced him. "My laird, the state of yer castle has never bothered you afore."

"Well it bothers me now. Do your duties Evan and fix it!"

Evan's eyes darkened but he remained silent. Rising from his chair, he yelled, "Stop fucking and get back to work!" Pushing back his chair, he stormed around the tables and pulled men off by their ears and kicked them. "Get dressed and go back to yer duties."

Disappointed moans blended with the clatter of dirty bowls being cleared from the tables. Scowls were shot at Evan, and Tremayne smiled. 'Twas only recent he made Evan the House Steward. Before then, Evan's station was a little more than a common servant. Taking orders from the likes of him did not sit well with the Campbell soldiers, some of them knights. But no one dared show their displeasure toward their laird for fear of reprisal.

Evan returned to his seat, grinning as if he commanded the soldiers through a great victory. Tremayne sensed the shift in Evan's aura, the older man was aroused. With a trembling hand, Evan slowly reached over to touch Tremayne's leg. His steward looked surreptitiously at him from beneath his eyelashes, lust glowing within his eyes.

"Continue with that course, and you would be fortunate to only lose your hands."

In midair, the steward withdrew.

"You know I do not enjoy a man's flesh," Tremayne growled. "Perhaps I should cut off one finger for every scar I have on my back."

Evan paled. "Master, I did not want to whip you. Yer mother commanded I teach you a lesson. She wanted to keep you hidden from the world. When you shouted to the people in the bailey, her secret was out."

"Having an heir should hold no shame," Tremayne growled through gritted teeth.

"I agree, but yer mother was…" Evan nervously looked around as if he would be struck by lightening. "…was vain."

"Aye, so you have told me. Her youth and beauty was all she cared about."

Evan added, "And do not forget sex and power." He slicked back oily brown hair and picked up his tankard, now filled with ale. "Speaking of yer mother, know you it is a full moon this eve?"

Tremayne resisted the urge to moan like his soldiers did earlier. "I am aware."

"Miss another moon and she will be greatly angered."

"You do not need to remind me." Tremayne nodded and smiled at the same pretty serving maid in the yellow kirtle as she lay down a bowl of lamb broth and bread. He imagined how her white thighs would quiver as he rammed into her from behind, and his cock rose in response.

"My laird, if you do not summon your mother, she will not tell you the name of yer father. Then all will be lost."

"She will not tell me anyway!" Tremayne pushed away from the table and rose abruptly. "If she was not already dead, I would kill her myself." He drank deeply from his ale and slammed it on the table. He pointed at the maid and then pointed upstairs. He faced Evan. "Perhaps with the blood of the witch, my mother will finally be appeased."

* * * * *

Gavenia settled into her saddle and tucked stray strands of bright golden hair beneath the coarse woolen cloak. Fortunately, the gate keeper was more concerned with the soldiers who entered than a lowly wench passing through the gates.

Her father would be furious if she was discovered riding alone. Even her brother was accompanied by soldiers when he rode outside the walls. In truth, they were his friends, but still, Callum was given more freedom than she because he was a man.

Kicking her horse into a fast gallop, Gavenia cherished the heady rush of rebellion and freedom. The hood of her cloak fell back and her hair flew wildly in the wind. The breeze cooled the heat of the sun upon her ivory skin while she rocked in rhythm to the horse's gait.

The troubles of the world disappeared when she rode into the forest. Its creatures, large and small, seem to welcome her as one of their own. All too soon, her secret glen came into view. Thick trees and shrubs surrounded the narrow valley, cradling a small blue pond. The smell of heather floated around her and she breathed deeply, her muscles relaxing.

Gavenia pulled her mount to a halt and swung off the saddle. The horse wandered to a thick patch of grass while she lowered herself near the pond's edge. Dipping her fingers in the cool water, she caused a ripple to affect the reflection of her face upon the surface. She wished she was not going to die from childbearing or be one of the last Celtic witches.

Why could she not be like the other maidens, giggling about men who trained in the fields? If not for this curse of knowing her death, she too, would be right beside them. Swaying her hips and licking her lips in hopes of catching the eye of a brave knight.

She needed to be touched, in an intimate way that made her feel like a woman. To feel the caress of a lover's hand or soft lips kissing every part of her body.

Gavenia sighed. Lying back on the grass, she unlaced her corset and her chemise, allowing the sun and breeze to touch her full breasts. She ran her fingers over her erect nipples, abandoning herself to the rising passion growing between her thighs. Her hands pulled up the folds of her skirt until she found her pantaloons. In one swift movement, she lifted her hips and pushed her undergarments to her knees, exposing her femininity.

Images of a naked man entering her chamber invaded her thoughts. Gavenia's head swam and her eyelids became heavy as erotic sensations swept over her body.

His raven hair touched the wide set of his shoulders as he stood like a statue, staring down at her with gleaming eyes of unspoken passion. His magnificent body was muscular and flawless, its strength barely controlled beneath a mask of wanting.

He lowered his mouth to hers and possessed her lips. She knew that she would be his forever and did not resist the tongue that plunged into her mouth.

He sat on the bed beside her. "Open yer legs wider," he ordered in a low voice full of wanting.

Oh, what a dream.

She did as he commanded, for the ache within her was unbearable. He dipped his long, rough fingers inside her moist lips. Her groan mingled with his.

"Do you like this?" he asked, cupping her breast with one hand and plundering his fingers inside her.

"Aye," she replied.

He pulled his hands away and Gavenia felt the cool breeze replace where it was once warm. She reached for him. "Please do not leave me."

He chuckled deep within his chest. "I move only to taste you."

Shifting, he settled between her legs. "Hmm, you smell of sexual yearning." He placed his hands on her inner thighs and opened her wider, exposing her to his intense perusal.

She moved closer to him, all inhibitions gone. "Taste me."

His eyes changed from blue to red as he kissed her moist center. His masterful tongue flicked her sensitive bud, then lapped at her entrance.

"I thirst for more," he said. "Give me more."

His savage hunger increased Gavenia's arousal. She arched her back as spasms of pleasure swept over her. Every inch of her body focused on the stimulation given by his tongue. The uncontrollable tremors inside were like liquid fire coursing beneath her skin. She could not believe how good she felt. She wanted to laugh, she wanted to cry.

By the time she opened her eyes, her breathing had returned to normal. The birds chirped and the breeze whistled passed her ears. The fantasy was broken, but not forgotten.

Gavenia lifted her pantaloons, pulled her skirt down and laced her clothes. She kneeled over the edge of the pond to splash water on her face. With the edges of her gown, she dabbed her skin dry and rose to watch the sun sink behind the mountain. It was getting late and soon she would be missed.

Swinging back into her saddle, she glanced down at the grassy area where she had laid. The image of the sensual man with red eyes burned into her memory. One day soon, she would escape again from her dreary castle to dream of her handsome lover.

* * * * *

Coira watched from behind the cover of thick trees as Lady Gavenia rode away. She brushed the leaves aside and stood at the pond. "Master, did you see that?"

Standing in his dark chamber, Tremayne looked into the scrying bowl that was filled with red wine. The image of Coira rippled in the ruby liquid. In the distance, Lady Gavenia expertly galloped her gray mare over the hill, toward Gleich Castle.

"Aye, her energies are powerful." His voice boomed through the still air around the pond, causing birds to take flight.

"Can we do that again? It was fun watching her squirm and moan."

Tremayne thought the same; his cock was hard and eager to plunge into Lady Gavenia like his tongue did in the illusion he controlled. He had no idea she would be so responsive to his seduction.

"Your duties have only just begun. Now go and befriend her. And Coira…"

"Aye, my laird?"

"Do not forget to steal the—"

"I will not fail you, Master."

Tremayne turned to find Evan standing at the doorway to his chamber, an unusual look upon his face. "What?"

The Celtic Witch and the Sorcerer 27

Evan sauntered in. "Why did you give Lady Gavenia pleasure when you could not gain energy from her being so far away?"

Tremayne refused to answer. His reasons were his alone. He need not explain them to anyone. "Perchance, what you should be asking me is why my steward feels the need to observe me while I am scrying?"

"Your mother never minded me watching her use her powers."

"I am not my mother!"

Grumbling beneath his breath, Evan turned and left the chamber.

Tremayne went to his chest and pulled out an ancient Scythian box made from bones, adorned with black, oval stones. Etched on the top was a drawing of his mother. Even obscure as it was, the ancient carver had captured her dark, sensual beauty. He placed the box next to his scrying bowl and opened the lid. Retrieving a black velvet cloth, he unwrapped the smooth material until a short, gold dagger was visible.

With a sigh, he took the dagger and sliced his hand, letting the blood drip into the bowl and blend with wine. Sinking his fingers into the liquid, he touched them to his lips and flicked the remaining droplets into the air.

The red liquid fell onto the rushes and from there, an image emerged of his mother. Her raven hair spilled around her shoulders, her ruby gown flared from an eerie wind within the chamber.

Lady Torella stretched her arms and smiled. When her hands finally dropped, she cupped her breasts and groaned with appreciation. "It has been too long since I have felt a mon touch my breasts."

Tremayne sat in his high-backed chair, his legs stretched before him. "Do not look to me to satisfy yer whims."

She scowled at him. "Hold thy wit! I am still yer mother."

Tremayne held his hand out and a goblet of wine flew from the trestle to his hand. "I am only too aware of that." Taking a sip, he stared at her over the rim. "Tell me, who is my father?"

Lady Torella avoided his gaze. "You will know when I am free from this hell."

"Time is running out, I must know now."

"It does not please me to give you the answer right now."

He rose and threw the goblet into the fireplace. "Do not vex me!"

Lady Torella stepped back, and then stood her ground. "Think you can scare me? I am dead; there is nothing you can do to me."

"Really?" he replied and took pleasure in watching her smug grin fade.

"Tremayne, I will tell you everything." His mother's voice shook with uncertainty. "Every answer you have been searching for all yer life, but first you must avenge me and set me free on Samhain's eve."

"Once I have captured the youngest Celtic witch, she will be sacrificed and you will be released from purgatory." Tremayne walked to the stone wall, picked up a long tallow from the fireplace ledge, and carried it over to where his mother stood. Her beautiful face was an intoxicating image, the same image many likened to him.

"This pleases me well." She smiled and went to kiss him on the lips, but he moved away.

"Good eve, Mother."

She went to open her mouth to speak, but he flicked wax from the candle into her image and she disappeared.

He walked to the window and stared at the full moon, the stars twinkled in the sky as if they knew a secret he did not.

When he released the Devil's sorceress, she would bring darkness and death to his people's land. But release his mother, he must.

He had no choice.

CHAPTER THREE

Gavenia awoke to the smell of fresh bread and honey. Her eyes fluttered open and focused on the wooden tray her brother swayed beneath her nose.

"Rise, my fair lady, the day awaits."

Gavenia groaned and struggled to sit up. Rubbing her eyes, she accepted the food from her brother and rested it on her lap. "Why are you so pleased this morn?"

"I have received a painting of my betrothed and she is beautiful," he chortled and sat on the bed next to her. Picking up the bread, he broke a piece and popped it into his mouth.

"You do not know that for sure. Maychance, Lady Vika MacEwen sent you a picture of someone else and, in sooth, she is really an old crone."

With his mouth full, he muffled, "I will not let you ruin my morn with yer cynical ranting." He jumped up from the bed and brushed the crumbs from his green tunic. "Besides, you should be worried about yer own neck."

Gavenia's head jolted up. "Why?"

"I saw you come in last eve from the stable."

"You did not tell Father?"

"Nae, I did not *tell* Father."

Gavenia released a sigh of relief.

"You should not be outside these walls alone. 'Tis not safe…especially for a lass."

With an unladylike scoff, she threw the bread at her brother. "Leave me now or you will soon squeal like a warthog!"

Callum chuckled and brushed his tunic again. "All right, my wee petal. But be warned, next time Father will be informed for yer own good."

The door opened and their mother entered just as Callum was leaving. He executed a courtly bow. "Milady mother."

Adela inclined her head. "My son, why are you in yer sister's chamber so early?"

"Someone needs to ruffle her awake in the morn," he said smoothly, his dimples deepening. "How else could she possibly begin her day otherwise?"

"Out!" Gavenia yelled from the bed.

"Gavenia, must you shriek like a common serf?" her mother admonished.

The door closed behind her brother and Gavenia swung her legs over the side of the high bed. "I pray yer pardon, Mother," she said in a low tone.

Gavenia walked over to the chair and table, then sat and passed the brush to her mother. Adela glided over to her and began to brush Gavenia's knotted locks. "I have acquired a maid for you."

"Pardon?"

"She is a little younger than you, but she tells me she is well experienced as a handmaiden to nobility." Her mother continued brushing.

"I do not need a maid."

"If you were not lonely, you would not feel the need to ride outside the walls unescorted," her mother's tone was flat, a sign that she was suppressing her vexation. Gavenia would rather receive a plague spot then be granted her mother's quiet stare.

Gavenia squeezed her eyes shut.

"Callum told you."

"Aye, and be thankful we did not inform yer father."

"Mother, I do not want a servant following me around, dogging my every step."

"Either you accept her, or I will have no choice but to tell yer father. And we both know he will discipline the poor gate keeper for being careless."

"Those are my alternatives?"

"Aye." Her mother handed the brush to her. "I will send the lass up immediately. She will sleep on a cot in here."

"Verily well, then." Gavenia watched her mother leave, then donned a gown of blue linen and tied the laces to the outer corset. Lifting her hair into a smock, she faced the door when it creaked open.

A petite, curvaceous maid walked into her chamber. Her green-brown eyes scanned Gavenia's belongings as if judging their worth. The way she moved spoke of sexual confidence, which left Gavenia wondering if her new maid would sneak out at twilight to dally with the soldiers. Gavenia guessed most men would covet such a beautiful woman, but something about her made her unattractive. Was it the dark circles under her eyes or the chilling presence she sensed behind them?

As if remembering her manners, Coira curtsied and Gavenia stared at the top of her head. Had she seen this maid before? She somehow seemed familiar.

Coira rose and smiled. "I am honored to serve you, milady."

Her tone was even, but everything inside Gavenia told her the maid spoke false. "Why is it you wish to serve me?" Gavenia bluntly asked.

"Who would not want to serve the great Celtic witch of the Roberts clan?"

Gavenia went to her bedside table and blew out her candle. "We do not allow word of our gifts to travel outside people we trust." Suspiciously, she faced Coira. "You are not from any of the Roberts allies, otherwise I would know of you. From where do you hail and how did you know that I am a witch?"

"I am daughter of Henderson from the lowlands, and Lady Adela told me of yer unique powers."

"When did…"

"Ah, I see you two are getting along." Her mother waltzed into the chamber and put her arm around Coira's shoulders. "Is she not lovely?"

The maid smiled in return as they both faced Gavenia. Gavenia returned a weak smile and nodded.

"Now, you two go on down to the hall," her mother said. "I had the cook prepare a special meal to break yer fast."

Gavenia resisted the urge to roll her eyes. If it was not bad enough to have someone watch over her, but her mother was treating her like a wee bairn again. She had to escape this place. All she wanted to do was travel to exotic lands, taste new food, witness different cultures. Instead she was trapped within the walls of *safety*. Confined because she was a witch and the world could not accept what they did not understand.

Coira walked out with her mother and Gavenia followed behind, listening to her mother answer the maid's questions. She asked about her mother's past, how she came to be the Lady of the castle, and if she had any enemies.

"Why do you want to know if we have enemies?" Gavenia interjected, descending down the spiral staircase.

Her mother stopped and looked back while Coira explained, "To be aware of one's enemy is to be forewarned."

"She is right, Gavenia," Her mother responded. "You must take heed of the danger that lurks not only outside our walls, but within."

Frustration boiled inside Gavenia. If she screamed right now, perhaps the maid would think her ill in the mind and would not accept the position.

"Come, come, Gavenia," her mother called at the bottom of the stairs. "We have a feast to prepare in less than a fortnight."

*****

The busy kitchen was stifling hot as the village servants rushed around preparing bread, sweetmeats, soups, and other dishes of delicacy. When the Roberts clan had a feast, all traveled from near and far to pay their respects to their chieftain, and to sample food from the best cooks in Scotland.

Gavenia rolled another log of dough between her palms. She had been making bread since dawn. Her wrists ached and her nose itched from the powdery grain. She did not mind helping the cooks; in truth, she enjoyed the smell of baking bread mixed with sweet spices from the pies. A nudge from behind almost had her land on the dough. Scowling, she turned around to see Callum smiling with his usual charm.

"What are you doing here?" she asked.

"Thought I would visit you and hide from yer friend, Coira." Callum brushed a finger across her face that was smeared with flour. "You are dirty."

Gavenia pushed his hand away and turned back to her batter. "Coira is no friend of mine. She only comes to my chamber late in the eve to sleep."

"Word through the barracks is she has visited every soldier here except me and Father." Callum leaned back against the table. "She will not leave me alone. I have told her I am betrothed, yet it does not matter to her."

The Celtic Witch and the Sorcerer

"I will talk to her."

"Will you?" Callum smiled and blinked his eyes at her as if he was innocent of the outcome.

"With one pledge."

"Anything for you, my wee petal."

Gavenia dusted her hands together and faced him. "Take me with you next time you go hunting. I want to be free of this oppressive castle."

He chuckled. "The hunt for the feast has passed. We have more than enough meat for our guests. Besides, you hate hunting."

"I do not care. I will close my eyes. I need to get away from mother and her constant talk of the *chosen one* and my obligation to procreate an heir." Gavenia leaned closer to whisper, "And Coira is always watching me when she is around. I think her eyes are too dark for one so young."

"She does not have the gift of integrity, that is for certain," her brother added.

"Mother is smitten by her. Perhaps she would prefer to have her for a daughter instead of me."

"That is false, sister. Do not say such things," Callum admonished. "Mother only wants what is best for you."

"Nae, Mother wants what is best for future Celtic magick."

Callum's eyes softened and he took her wrist to lead her away. She resisted. "Wait, I have not finished this bread…"

"Let the cooks finish it. You need a respite."

Gavenia followed her brother out of the stifling kitchen into the cool bailey. With a mischievous grin, she rubbed her floury hands on Callum's tunic and he jumped away from her.

Brushing the powder off, he growled, "And I was about to show you a secret."

"Pray tell, what secret could you have that I do not already know?"

They walked around the side of the castle and came to an alcove where the battlements joined the wall of the castle. "What are we doing here?"

"This is the secret." Callum pointed at the wall.

"Intriguing," she said with sarcasm. "A dead end."

Callum gently pushed her to the side and pulled a loose brick from the battlements. A small door opened, affording entrance to the outside.

Gavenia gasped and peeked through the doorway. "How did you come by this?"

"Father showed me when I was a lad. He said if we were ever under siege, it was my duty to see you and Mother to safety." Callum grasped her shoulders and turned her to face him. "You must never tell anyone of this passage and only use it when I am with you."

"I will, I will."

"Pledge to me you will not go out alone."

"Pray, stop worrying, Brother. I will be all right."

Callum did not look convinced, but she knew he trusted her. Throwing her arms around his waist, she hugged him tightly. "Thank you."

"I have a sour feeling about this now."

"Come, let us go for a brisk walk." She pulled Callum through the passage.

He laughed. "Vixen!"

From behind the corner, Coira watched the brother and sister disappear beyond the passage, the wall closing with a grating noise.

"So, the little bird wishes to be free of her gilded castle." Lifting a shawl over her head she hastened toward the stables to find her horse. Beneath her breath, she uttered, "Lady Gavenia will soon find a cage she canna escape."

CHAPTER FOUR

Tremayne sat in his chair watching three beautiful women making love upon his fur-lined bed. The nymphs writhed with passion, licking and kissing each other in a triangle. Although their energy was intoxicating, he was unstirred to join them. The image of Lady Gavenia played in his mind. Her sweet, pink lips called to him, asking him to touch her. Her curly, golden hair glistened in the sunlight as if spun from the finest silk. Skin so creamy, he yearned to run his tongue over every inch of her body. Tremayne felt his manhood rise at the thought. He was just about to reconsider his decision and join the ladies when a knock sounded at the door.

"Enter!"

Coira rushed in and kneeled at his feet. "My lord, I have news of Lady Gavenia."

Tremayne edged forward. "Continue."

"She has a way to escape the watchful eye of her family."

"Know you when she will leave?"

"I will make it so on the eve of the great feast. I believe she will be driven to seek solace through a cloaked passage."

Tremayne rose, the bulge beneath his kilt was in line with Coira's face. Her eyes shone with lust. "Allow me to ease yer burden," she purred and began to run her hands up his legs.

"Do not touch me unless I give permission." He pushed her away and she fell to the side. "Besides, I have three lovely ladies here." He walked to the edge of the bed. "Come to me," he commanded the women on the bed.

They scrambled to kneel side by side upon the furs. Slowly, he waved his hand over their faces, and they transformed into the image of Lady Gavenia.

"As you can see, Coira, I have no need of yer services. Return to Gleich Castle and make sure Lady Gavenia is unescorted on the eve of the feast."

Tremayne lay on the bed and allowed the nymphs to enjoy his body. They would not be as satisfying as the real lady, but they would do until he captured the witch and plowed inside her.

* * * * *

"May I come in?" Gavenia's father stood at the doorway to her chamber.

His flaxen hair was tied back at the nape and he wore his training tunic, kilt and sword. Even at the age of forty-nine winters, the chieftain had an angelic face with the stature of a young knight. Many a time had passed when she went to the back of her father, thinking it was Callum. It was nary a wonder that her mother and father were still deeply in love. She too wished to have such an endearing love.

Nodding her head, she motioned her father to enter.

He threw his arms around her. "It does so gladden my heart to see you. I know I have been distracted of late. The duties of a chieftain hold much of my attention."

"I understand, Father." Gavenia padded across the fresh rushes to the wardrobe and pulled on a pair of yellow slippers that matched her primrose gown. "Have guests arrived early for the great feast on the morrow?"

"Aye, yer mother wishes you to come down and greet them." Her father shifted uneasily as if he had more to say but could not find the words.

Gavenia took pity on him. "Pray tell, what it is she wanted you to put forth?"

Her father gave her a crooked smile. "I detest how you can read me so easily. 'Tis bad enough yer mother does the same."

"Father, what did you want to say?" Gavenia urged, her tone softening.

"You must decide on a husband at the great feast. We have invited all the noblemen in Scotland, so there will be many choices, and…"

"Nae." Gavenia turned away from him and sat on the windowsill to look at the full moon shining over the village.

Her father followed her and leaned against the wall.

"Your mother had a hard life by herself and she became a recluse, fearing people before she even met them."

"That is my mother. I am not her," Gavenia whispered, resisting the urge to cry over the same story she had heard many times.

"Nae, you are not. You have had the sanctuary of loved ones to surround you and protect you." Her father touched her shoulders. "I do not want to see you lonely."

If only she could tell her father of her future, of the death that awaited her. Taking a deep breath, she responded, "I do not need yer protection and I do not need a mon." A silent tear fell down her cheek. She tilted her head away from her father and absently wiped her cheek. "My powers will keep me safe."

"You canna rely on yer powers for protection."

Gavenia held her hand out the window. In the distance a star rested on her palm. She spoke to it. "Grant me thy brightness."

The star fell from the sky and traveled through distance to rest on her palm. Its size remained small as if it were still in the sky.

"I can bring you a star from heaven, change the weather with a few words, and raise our crops to be bountiful without a drop of water, and yet, you still do not trust me."

Her father picked up her other hand and kissed it tenderly. "I trust you, my daughter. It is the dark forces out there that I do not trust." He sighed and turned. Walking to the door, he pivoted. "How did you get me off the subject of marriage?"

Gavenia granted him a sheepish smile.

"It is time to accept yer duty." He shook his head regretfully, his eyes full of sorrow. "Either you choose a mon at the great feast or I will. Chosen one or no chosen one. Come this harvest, you will be wed." He turned and left silently.

Smothering a groan, she felt ill with despair. She stood up from the window sill and blew the star off her hand. "Return to yer place in the sky."

The star flew out the window and upwards. She watched its path, wishing she could escape so easily.

Gavenia jumped when she felt a presence behind her. Coira stood by the bed, a dark shadow passed over her eyes and then it was gone.

"Is something amiss?" Coira asked.

"Nae. I was going to ask you the same thing."

The maid laughed and her eyes began to sparkle once more. She trailed her hands up and down the bed curtains, her pink lips pursed. "I am bored with this place. Nothing exciting ever happens."

"There is the great feast on the morrow."

"And then what? Do you not ever get bored?"

"Sometimes."

Coira hastened over to her and grabbed her hands. "Let us visit my aunt in the Edinburgh. There are so many wonderful things to do in town. There are festivals, plays, and lots of markets with pretty linen to be bought. They say the people of Edinburgh build high houses close to the protection of the castle. 'Tis an unusual sight to be seen."

"I do not know."

"We can leave at midnight, when everyone is asleep, dreaming of the great feast."

Gavenia shifted on her feet.

Coira added, "Ye have all the time in the world to stay in the castle and have fat babies. Why not live now before you are caged into marriage."

"Aye, caged. That is all I will ever be." Gavenia's heart skipped a beat. It was her life and if she was to be married and have a babe, then at least she would have visited one large town before she died. "We leave this eve. Be ready and I will get us out of the keep."

Coira smiled. "We are going to have so much fun." Her maid opened the door.

"Where are you going?" Gavenia's mind was in a whirl of preparations for her trip to freedom. "Tarry not with the soldiers."

"There is something I must do before we leave, but I will return before midnight. I promise I will not tell a soul." Coira smiled again and closed the door behind her.

Gavenia used the time to write a note to her family, explaining that she needed time before settling down with a husband. She hoped that she did not disappoint them, but it was something she needed to do. Gavenia implored them not to worry. After all, she did have her powers and would only use them if she felt threatened. She would return before spring to see to the crops.

Folding a few gowns into a bag along with a handful of gold, she hid her belongings beneath her bed and left her chamber with a smile.

Come midnight, she would be on her way to following her dreams. No persisting mother, overprotective father and annoying brother to remind her daily of her duty to good magick. She would face that storm when she returned.

* * * * *

Like a cat, Coira entered the chamber of Laird and Lady Roberts. Day by day she searched their possessions undetected, yet she returned without satisfaction. She must find it now. Time had run out. She twirled around in frustration and then stood still, pursing her lips. Where could it be? Why did she even bother doing this for her master? He had not made love to her since…since he sent her to follow Lady Gavenia. Argh! Lady Gavenia with her lovely golden hair and lovely ruby lips. Why was he obsessed with the woman? She did not know. Maybe, once she returned to her master's side, he would have missed making love to her and would take her back into his chamber again.

For now, she had to find the…

There was only one place left she had not searched. Falling to her knees, she looked under the bed. Her heart leaped into her throat. Hidden beneath was a chest. She pulled out the slender box.

Brushing off the dust, the lid opened without opposition. "Foolish witch should have at least locked the chest."

Within the confines sat a thick ancient book with *Dark Magick* written in gold across the cover. It had belonged to her master's mother, Lady Torella, and now it would be returned to the rightful sorcerer. Tucking it into a leather sack, she rose and hastily left the chieftain's chamber.

Closing the door behind her, she jolted at the touch on her shoulder.

"Why were you in my parent's chamber?"

Coira turned to see Sir Callum. A frown marred his heavenly features. He studied the sack at her side. Her heart beat loudly within her ears. "I...I...Lady Gavenia requested I fetch a book from her mother's chamber."

"Did she now?" The handsome knight looked unconvinced. "Let me see the book my sister requested." He went to reach for the sack, but Coira shifted to the side.

Coira moistened her lips slowly, drawing his attention to her tongue. A lustful light flitted across his sea-green eyes. She placed her hand on his chest and pushed up on her toes, her mouth inches away from his.

"Forget yer sister. Why have you been avoiding me?"

His erection pressed against her belly and she edged closer to him, using her body as friction. Although she wanted to kiss him, she instead teased him longer by her nearness.

"You know why," he answered, remaining still.

Sir Callum's breath smelled of sweet wine and it drove her wild with wanting. *Kiss me*, she screamed in her head.

Suddenly, he grasped her waist and held her tight. His lips crushed hers with passion. If she was not so aroused, she would have gloated with victory.

She had him!

Fiddling with the door handle behind her, it opened and they stumbled into the master's chamber. He scooped her up into his arms and threw her onto the bed. Coira shoved the sack off her shoulder and threw it to the side. With hurried hands, she lifted her blue gown over her head, her gaze unwavering on the golden-haired knight undressing before her. His brawny physique was as hard as stone and his impressive cock nestled against crisp hair. He stood over her, his fists clenched at his sides.

"This is what you wanted, was it not?" His tone was confident, daring her to disagree.

Coira licked her dry lips again, her body tingled with anticipation. "Aye."

"Then take it!" he ordered.

Crawling to the edge of the bed, she grasped his member with one hand and covered it with her mouth. She engulfed part of his length and groaned, enjoying the feel of his warm shaft gliding along her tongue. She pulled him out and placed a kiss on the smooth round tip, then ran her pursed lips down the length. Lifting his member, she sucked on the soft sacs hanging below, then licked from the base to the tip again.

He moaned. "You like sucking cock."

"Aye," she breathed and returned to fucking him with her mouth.

His body stiffened and Coira knew he was close. He pushed her away and she lay on the bed, her legs open so he might see all her glory. Men were usually uncontrollable when given such a view, but the knight only awarded her a wicked grin. Slowly, he kneeled between her thighs and placed the pad of his thumb inside her mouth. Closing her eyes she sucked on the salty taste of his skin. Dear Lord, even his fingers tasted good.

Taking his glistening thumb, he pressed it between her legs and ran it down her moist lips, circling her sensitive bud. His index finger slid inside of her, while his thumb continued the stimulation on the outside. Coira squirmed with ecstasy, pushing against his hand to enter further inside. He held his body away from hers. So masculine and in control, it drove her insane with desire.

She grabbed his forearms and ordered, "I want you inside me!"

Sir Callum smiled and licked his fingers as if he dipped them in sweet honey. Falling over her, he propped himself up on his elbows, his muscular arms bulging on either side of her head. She opened her legs wider to

The Celtic Witch and the Sorcerer

accommodate his size, waiting for him to enter and end the torment of her arousal.

Swaying his hips, the tip of his cock lightly rubbed against her wetness. She arched toward him, but he pulled away, teasing her.

"Please, I need you inside."

"Why were you in this chamber?" he whispered, as if citing poetry.

"Hmm?" Surely he was not asking her that now? Not while she was desperate for him.

"Why were you in this chamber?" he repeated. Slowly, his wide helmet dipped inside.

"I...I told you. To get a book." She arched toward him again, but he shifted backward. Saint Mary, she needed more of him.

"Did my sister really send you?"

He slid his throbbing erection further into her receptive body. Mad with wanting, obsession overrode everything else.

"Nae." She said without thinking, her body driving her to distraction. Sweat matted her hair, her breathing increased. Right now she would kill to have him completely impale her. Why did he not take her? This was torture of the worst kind.

"Who sent you?"

He pushed in and out of her, but with only half his length, leaving her desires unsated. She tried to draw him near, her nails scratching his back, but he resisted.

"Who sent you?" he asked, this time probing deep within her core. She groaned with ecstasy, her body betraying her with heightened arousal. He pulled out from her, only to thrust hard inside of her once more, and then out.

"Who?" he demanded.

"Laird...laird..."

"Aye?"

"Laird..." Without another word, she reached her peak, even without his cock within her. She clutched at him, pleading for him to fill her.

Cursing, Callum plunged in, riding her pleasure until he released his own.

Every ounce of their passion was spent before he collapsed beside her. The strain of resisting the vixen had his skin sleek with sweat. It was worth it to gain a little information from Coira. What laird had asked the lass to steal from his mother?

Rolling to the side of the bed, he picked up her sack and pulled out an old, thick book titled, *Dark Magick*. He didn't know his mother kept a book like this in her chamber.

A noise sounded behind him and he turned to find a large metal urn crashing down on his head, then blackness.

Coira picked up the book from the floor and stepped over Sir Callum's body.

"That's for taking so long to fuck me!"

CHAPTER FIVE

Gavenia spent most the eve avoiding her mother and mingling with clan members she had not seen since last harvest. She was thankful her mother did not bring over any men to be introduced, thus allowing Gavenia to enjoy the eve before retiring.

She lay on her soft bed. Her body was exhausted, but her mind was alert with excitement. She must force herself to rest while she could. At midnight, she would escape the castle and ride through the night.

Slowly, very slowly, her eyelids lowered and she drifted into sleep.

"I have been waiting for you to slumber," his deep voice held a note of tenderness.

Gavenia sat up. Her sleeping chemise changed from white to black, its delicate fabric dipping low to expose the inner curve of her breasts. She looked up at the handsome stranger standing over her bed. It was the mysterious man of her dreams. Just the nearness of him made her body tingle with desire. His hair was as black as midnight and it fell in soft waves to his shoulders. His bare torso gleamed from the glow of the fireplace while black chausses hung low on his hips. Dark eyes captured her gaze and held it as if she was in a trance. She feared him, but was attracted to him at the same time.

She trembled from the force of her body's cravings for this man. She had never felt this way before and it frightened her. This was only a dream, right? So why should she worry? Why resist her cravings for this figment of her imagination? After all, she could not become pregnant from a dream.

The man smiled and lay down beside her. Gathering her into his arms, he molded her curves readily into his own contours and murmured, "Everything will be all right."

Gavenia studied every inch of his face while the hardness of his warm body gave her comfort. His face was so beautiful and noble, with an aristocrat nose and eyebrows. His strong jaw line was clean-shaven while his lips…oh sweet Goddess, his lips were full and soft. They smiled at her, knowing everything she was thinking.

"I do not usually like to kiss, but I find myself eager to explore yer mouth again," he confessed, his voice low, sensual.

Gavenia's heart flipped in response. He could ask anything from her, and she would agree. When his appreciative gaze roamed over her, she felt feminine and desirable. All her barriers toward men instantly fell.

He was meant to be her lover, and she, his.

Holding her hand to his chest, he gradually lowered his head and claimed her lips. Soft and tender, he tentatively explored the insides of her mouth, then deepened the kiss as her ardor grew. Their tongues made love with a savage hunger, each desiring to be closer and closer, merging their bodies, but he was still too far away. She needed him inside her, to complete her. She needed more of him.

Breaking from his lips was unbearable. She lifted her head to plead, "Touch me."

He fiercely returned to kissing her as his warm hand eased the black satin chemise over her breasts. Gently, his hand circled her breasts while his thumb ran across her sensitive nipples. She pressed closer to him, her skin on fire. She wanted more of his touch, heat and tongue.

"You are intoxicating," he murmured.

He bent to kiss her breasts when the chamber door slammed open.

"Gavenia, get dressed, it is time to…" Coira rushed in and came to an abrupt halt. "I am sorry, I am sorry!" Fear laced her apology and she dropped to the ground on her knees.

Her lover turned toward the intrusion and growled. The threatening sound sent shivers down Gavenia's spine. He turned to face Gavenia, and his eyes softened. "Come to me," he whispered, then disappeared into a shadow.

Gavenia shook her head after a wave of dizziness threatened to overwhelm her. She sat up and looked down at her gown, it was white again, but her breasts were exposed.

Coira lifted herself from the rushes and began packing as if nothing happened.

Gavenia felt her forehead, the skin was warm to the touch, yet the rest of her body was chilled.

"Wake up sleepy. It is time we left," Coira chirped.

"Was I asleep?" She swung her legs over to the side of the bed.

"Aye, that must have been some dream. You were moaning." Coira finished packing and stood at the end of the bed. Her smile did not reach her eyes, but Gavenia shrugged it away. She was probably tired, like herself. Gavenia did not feel she got any rest at all.

"I will don my green riding gown, then we can go."

Coira's eyes darted around the chamber, averting Gavenia's gaze. Her maid opened the door and peeked out, her jittery moves making Gavenia nervous.

"You must make haste, milady."

Gavenia finished dressing and pulled her sack out from beneath her bed. Taking the note she had inked before, she left it on her bed. "I am ready," she said, her heart beating faster at the thought of traveling through the country. Finally, an adventure all of her own.

Coira nodded. "Go ahead and wait for me in the stables. I will meet you there."

Gavenia nodded. "Aye, it would be easier to sneak over the soldiers sleeping in the Great Hall if we left separately."

Coira watched her ladyship leave with a travel bag slung over her shoulder. Her smile fell into a sneer. It took so much energy to be nice to that spoiled aristocrat. Opening the chamber door, she returned to the bed and picked up the note. Opening it, she read its contents and scoffed with disgust.

With the flick of her hand, she threw the note into the fireplace and turned her back on the flames.

"Soon milady, you will get a taste of what it is like to be less than a peasant."

* * * * *

Coira did not look surprised when Gavenia opened the secret doorway to the outside world. Unwilling to read more into her companion's actions, Gavenia lightened the mood with small chatter. She asked her where her aunt lived in Edinburgh and would she be put out if they visited without word? Coira's response was either one syllable or a vacant nod. Perhaps her maid did not fare well on little sleep. If truth be told, she wished she had stayed in her wondrous dream a little longer.

After riding their horses through most of the eve, Coira stopped her mount in a small clearing. Trees and shrubs surrounded them like a wall.

"We can rest here until dawn. Try to get some sleep," Coira ordered, her tone brusque.

Relieved, Gavenia dismounted, tied her light gray palfrey to a tree and then unrolled a blanket from the back of her horse. Dropping her sack next to Coira's makeshift fire, she walked over to the other side of the camp. Every limb in her body screamed for rest, and once the blanket was on the ground, Gavenia collapsed upon it and went straight to sleep.

What seemed like only moments later, she awoke after hearing a noise. The hair on the back of her neck stood on end. It was still dark, before dawn. She sat up and scanned the area. No other movement from the trees came. She looked over at her maid, but Coira was gone, along with her bag. A few of Gavenia's gowns were strewn about the ground, her gold vanished.

"Coira?" she called, but no answer. "Coira!"

Something was wrong. Something was terribly wrong. She could feel it in her very spirit. Suppressing the urge to panic, she rose and gathered her gowns. She didn't know which direction she needed to go; she just knew she had to make haste.

Gavenia stopped picking up her gowns and stood still. The surrounding forest was dead silent. The only sound was her heavy breathing. Her heart beat increased, dread threatened to overwhelm her. Evil was nearby. She could not shake the feeling.

She had to leave.

Now!

Dropping her belongings, she leapt onto her saddle and sunk her heels into the horse's flanks. Jolting forward, unseen branches whipped at her arms and face, her mount racing carelessly through the woods.

Suddenly a sound of hoof beats came from behind.

She was being chased.

Lowering her head closer to her mount, she urged her horse to a greater speed. Low hanging trees threatened to dismount her, yet she dodged each one. She managed to look around. A dark horseman was dangerously close, effortlessly riding a black steed.

He pulled out a whip from his saddle and it glowed bright orange. Gavenia's breath caught in her throat. The whip couldna be for her, could it? What did he want? Why could he not leave her alone? She must keep her head.

Keep riding.

Faster. Faster.

The horseman covered more ground than her exhausted palfrey. She needed help and now. Mumbling a spell, a lightening bolt came from the cloudless sky and it struck the ground before the horseman. His large stallion glided over it.

"What horse is not afraid of lightening?"

She faced the front. A branch almost took her head off before she ducked.

"If I canna stop you with fire, maybe I can stop you with ice." Uttering another spell, the clouds gathered and rain poured down, it then turned to hail. Large rocks of ice fell from the sky, hitting the horseman, but he continued on as if the hail were flowers.

Gavenia looked around again. Not only did he not slow, he was gaining on her. Her mount was no match for his warhorse.

The horseman looped the lasso in the air again; the orange light brightened the forest with an eerie glow.

Gavenia's pulse increased with fear and she urged her tired mount for more speed. He was almost upon her.

She heard the whip crack and flinched.

A tight bind wrapped around her waist and arms. Suddenly, she was jerked off her mount and into the dirt with a thud, knocking the breath from her lungs. It took her a moment to shake the darkness from her head.

The hail she cursed the stranger with was now falling on her. She mumbled a spell to stop the weather. Suddenly, the lasso around her waist tightened, cutting into the flesh on her arms.

The horseman stood over her, his face in the shadows. "Confounding witch!"

He gathered her into his arms and threw her over the rump of his horse. Gavenia went to chant another spell.

"The chain you wear is cursed. With every spell you utter, it will tighten until it breaks through yer arms and squeezes the very breath from yer body," he warned, his tone rough and cold. Swinging into his saddle, he turned back to her and whispered in her ear. "I suggest you keep yer mouth shut."

The vehemence in his voice made Gavenia shiver. She had so many questions, but was afraid to ask in case the chain tightened further with the mere sound of her voice.

The sunrise streaked across the sky as his mount spurred into a swift gallop. The chain cut into her skin with every movement of the horse, and blood oozed down her arms.

Gavenia closed her eyes. *Please, Mother, wake up. I need you!*

CHAPTER SIX

Gavenia's frightened voice echoed through the chamber and Adela jolted awake. Rising from the bed, she ran barefoot down the hallway into her daughter's chamber. It was empty and cold, the chamber's fire having died long ago so that only ashes remained in the stone cave.

Where was she?

Adela held her palms outward and chanted, "Give me the vision, I seek only one. Show me my daughter and I will be done."

Adela opened her eyes, but no vision appeared. She chanted the spell again and still no vision. Her magick must be blocked. But how?

She closed her eyes and chanted, "I call upon the Triple Goddess of sun, earth and moon. Goddess Triana, come to me, I beg of you."

A white mist floated through the window and transformed into an alluring blue lady. Her white hair floated around her shoulders as if she was beneath the water. Her full eyes shined completely green, her lips were black.

"How can I assist you, milady?" a lilting voice asked.

"Where is my daughter? Is she well? Why did she leave? Why can I not summon a vision of her?"

Goddess Triana held her hand up to halt the questions. "Lady Gavenia has been captured."

Adela's hand covered her mouth, her worst fears being realized. Tears threatened to sting her eyes. She took a large breath and calmed herself. She must not loose time to emotions. She would cry later.

"Where...where has she been taken and how do we rescue her?" Adela asked, her voice shaking with dread.

"I cannot tell you."

"Why not?" Panic welled in her throat.

"You must not rescue your daughter or else misfortune will befall your family."

"Nae! I have to go to her. She needs me."

"You have been warned." The Goddess faded from sight.

Adela collapsed on the bed. What should she do? What could she do?

The echo of heavy boots vibrated against the stones in the hallway and Adela watched her son enter the room. He rubbed his head. His usual handsome face was screwed up in pain. He went to Coira's bed and kicked the empty mattress. "Where is that bitch!"

"Coira is gone," Adela sobbed, unable to hold back any longer, tears streamed down her face.

"No need to cry about it."

"And so is yer sister."

Callum's eyes shot open. His voice was firm, determination straightening his body. "Then we go after her."

"Nae, Goddess Triana has warned me not to interfere. Yer sister must go through this lesson alone."

"Mother, she could be in danger."

"Even if we were to go after her, I do not know where she is." Adela rose and grabbed her son's arm. "Come, we must tell yer father."

Her husband paced the floor of their chamber. Phillip's voice was gravel from being woken. "How did she get out? The gate has been closed for the eve."

Callum lowered his head. "I showed her the secret passage."

"You did what?"

"Do not blame him," Adela interjected. "Gavenia is a stubborn lass, she would have found a way."

"She is all alone out there," Phillip hissed.

"Oh, if only she was," Callum said cryptically. They both looked at him expectantly. "I wager Coira is with her."

"Why does that cause concern?" Adela asked.

"I caught her last eve stealing a book from yer chamber."

Adela gasped. "Pray tell it is not the book of *Dark Magick*?"

"Aye."

"She is in more danger than we thought," Phillip declared. "Gavenia is naïve to evil. We must go after her."

"We canna, my husband." She touched Phillip's arm. "Goddess Triana has warned me not to rescue her or else doom will befall us all."

"We canna just leave her," Phillip raged.

"Whatever happens now is fate and you canna fight that," Adela explained. She caressed her husband's face, her eyes pleading for him to understand, even when she did not.

He kissed her hand, pain mirrored in his eyes.

"Then she is on her own?" Callum asked.

"Aye," Adela whispered, "she is on her own."

* * * * *

The muscles in Gavenia's stomach were bruised from balancing her weight on the back of her captor's stallion. She was glad she had not eaten anything since yesterday. The contents of her stomach would have been thrown up with the constant rocking of the horse's hind legs. The only view she was in a position to see was her captor's boot, horse's flank and the ground. Thick hair swished over her head, blocking most of the view of the ground. The sun beat down upon her fair skin and without the protection of her long hair, the back of her neck started to burn. This was undignified for a lady!

"Pray pardon…" she choked, a strand of hair went into her mouth. Sputtering it out with her tongue, she shook her head. "Pray pardon," she said louder. "Do you mind if we stop so I can see to the necessities?"

The only answer was the clip clop of his horse's hooves.

"I said," her voice rose louder, "I need to stop!"

No answer.

Another jolt came from the horse's rump when it stumbled over a rock. Gavenia groaned as the horse's rough backside pressed against her bladder. If he didn't stop soon, his damn warhorse was going to be soaked with urine.

She was about to sting him with choice words when the horse walked over a bridge. The muddy ground looked to be well traveled. A grating noise of a gate sounded nearby. The horse stepped backward and then forward over a wooden plank.

Gavenia lifted her head but her view was obstructed by her hair. She shook her head to see a village of filthy peasants watching her be paraded along the path. This was not the adventure she had in mind when leaving Gleich Castle. She should have told someone she was leaving. Where was Coira? Perhaps she got scared and returned to the castle. Even now, her father and brother could be mounting a search for her. This man would rue the day he kidnapped one of the Robert's clan. She groaned again when the horse sidestepped. Dear Goddess! Her bladder was about to explode.

Her captor halted the horse and swung down, keeping his back to her. Gavenia lifted her head to peer through a wall of blond hair to see his face. She wanted to see the heathen who would be killed when her father rescued her. Alas, he kept his back to her and gave two guards orders.

Turn around, turn around, she commanded in her mind.

As if reading her thoughts, he slightly turned to look at her from the corner of his eye, though, not enough for her to make out his features. A hint of a smile from the corner of his lips was all she saw before he ran up the stairs. She assumed the stairs led to a castle, but she could not see for sure in her position.

Two rough sets of hands pulled her over the horse and carried her like a sack of wheat. They took her to the side of the castle and dropped her on damp grass, then turned their backs. Was she supposed to relieve herself while they stood close by? The orange lasso bound her arms to her side, so she could only lift her gown a small measure. Unwilling to miss the opportunity for relief, she squatted and did her best to keep her gown dry. When she was finished, she hoisted herself up. The guards went to carry her again, but she stepped back.

"I can walk," she quickly assured them.

They shrugged and grabbed both her arms and led her toward a single tower. The only entrance was a weathered oak door. They pushed her through and led her up a steep, spiral staircase. One missed step and she would tumble down to her death. The muscles in her legs burned by the time she reached the top.

Breathless, she asked, "Is it necessary for this chamber to be so high?"

The guards smothered their smiles and creaked open the wooden door to a lone chamber. She went inside and turned to see the door slam close. "I take a goblet of French wine before sunset."

The guards laughed, then the distant thudding of boots echoed down the stairway.

Bravado failed her once she scanned the high dungeon. Unlike the Robert's dungeons, this one was filthy. The old rushes were soiled. A brittle chair sat in the corner, its feeble, scratched wood threaded with gray mold. She wondered if it had the strength to hold a person without collapsing. A bed of straw lay on the ground in the corner, its mass probably filled with rats.

Why was she here? And where was here? She had never traveled far from Gleich Castle, so her knowledge of direction was limited. She hoped Coira was all right and did not fall foul to her captor and his guards. The lump that lingered in her throat was hard to swallow. Her only hope was that her maid had escaped to send help.

*****

Coira lay naked on the bed, her legs open to allow her master full view of her womanhood when he entered his chamber. Where was he? Coira heard the commotion below some time ago and still he had not sought her out.

Rolling over the side of the bed, she pulled out the black book from her sack. If he did not come for her, he would certainly come for this book. Opening the old cover, she explored the yellow pages, her eyes widening at the curses of dark magick. If she had the power, she would use it against Lord Tremayne. Have him see to her every need instead of the other way around. She hated how he could command her with such cruelty and she would obey, then beg for more. Since he had sent her to Gleich Castle, he had been more interested in the Lady Gavenia than her.

Why did he bother with the spoiled witch when he could have his sex maid anytime he wanted? Perchance he sought ransom? Either way, he would soon bore of the maiden lady and come back to her. All men did.

The chamber door opened and her master entered. He peeled off his damp tunic and threw it to the floor. His gaze then shifted to her and darkened. Coira remained still, unsure of his mood. He kneeled on the bed and leaned over her. Finally, she was going to receive incredible pleasure only he could give. She opened her arms.

He snatched the book from her lap and closed it shut.

"Never touch this book again!" He turned to sit on the edge of the bed, his solid back to her. His head tilted when he began to flick through the pages.

Coira smiled and crawled over to him. She desperately wanted to put her arms around his neck and press her breasts against his back, but she knew to touch him without his consent would mean being banished from his chamber for a whole season. A mistake she would never make again.

Instead she lay down beside him, her hands over her head to make her breasts available and appealing. She waited for him to look. But still he ignored her. She sighed, adverting her gaze.

Goddamn it, look!

She sighed louder.

"Get off my bed," he commanded without breaking his focus on the book.

Pouting, Coira rose and swiftly dressed. Anger fueled her movements as she shoved on her slippers. It took all her effort not to scream at him.

"What do you plan to do with Lady Gavenia?" she asked.

Finally, his head jolted up at the mention of *her* name and his eyes brightened with lust. He used to have that same look when she was new to his chamber. Now they were dull when he looked upon her. Curse Lady Gavenia!

"'Tis of no consequence to you, Coira. Go down to the kitchens and see if they need help." He returned to reading.

Kitchens! She seethed with humiliation and fury.

The Celtic Witch and the Sorcerer 61

This was all Lady Gavenia's doing.

She went to storm out of his chamber, but halted when she saw a blade on the table by the door. With her back to her master, she stole the dagger.

CHAPTER SEVEN

"Argh!" Gavenia struggled with the evil contraption around her waist and arms. She rubbed her back against the damp wall to loosen the tight hold, but it did not budge. There was nothing in the dungeon she could use to dislodge the orange chain.

Her knees buckled and she collapsed to the floor, the taste of bile in her mouth.

When she escaped these binds, she would shower upon her captor a year of rain and thunder, flooding his keep and destroying his crops. A furious scream lodged in her throat. She fought again within the tether, her strength depleting as she continued to resist.

Gavenia slumped, her heart aching with hopelessness. A flood of tears broke through the last shreds of control. She rested her forehead on the filthy rushes, her long hair covering the humiliation on her heated face. When were Father and Callum going to come for her? Mentally, she calculated how long it would be before they reached her. If Coira fled home and summoned her father, it would not be until two moons at least before they arrived. Gavenia groaned. She did not think she could last much longer with the chain cutting into her skin.

Echoes of footsteps on the stairway came closer. Awkwardly, Gavenia pushed to her feet and raised her chin. She would not show these heathens that she was afraid. If only she had a hand to wipe the tears from her face. Tilting her head, she rubbed her cheek against her shoulder. It did not erase the moist path on her face, but it would have to do.

The keys rattled in the lock.

Her stomach clenched tight, her palms sweating.

Be brave, Gavenia, be brave.

The oak door swung open.

"Coira!" Gavenia smiled with relief. "How did you get past the guards? No matter." Gavenia turned around. "Undo this vile chain. Quickly."

Gavenia waited for her to approach, why was she taking so long? "I canna believe you are rescuing me by yourself. I hope you sent word to my father. Hurry, Coira, we do not have much time before the castle will be alert."

Silence from behind made Gavenia uncomfortable. She turned to look at her maid. Coira stood in the doorway, a long dagger gripped in her hand. Her hazel eyes blazed with contempt.

"Coira?"

"He is obsessed with you," she accused in a low voice, her lip curling into a scowl. "I know not why. Look at you...you are pale and slim. Too weak and inexperienced to give him the passion he needs."

"Coira?" Gavenia whispered. Her heart hammered in her chest when realization sunk through. "You betrayed me? Why?"

"Betrayed is a word for friends. I was never yer friend," she spat. Holding her dagger high, she stalked toward Gavenia.

Gavenia turned to face her and stepped back until she was flush against the wall. "Your death will be painful, Coira. I have foreseen it!" Gavenia watched her falter, her eyes blinking.

"I care not for yer prophesy."

Gavenia began to chant a protection spell, but the tether around her arms tightened until she felt her ribs were going to break. She fell to the ground, breathless.

Coira grabbed a handful of her hair. Gavenia screamed as her hair was pulled tightly from her scalp, her eyes stinging with tears. The cutting sound of the blade sickened her as soft locks fell to the ground. There was nothing she could do. Her hair was ruined.

Coira stood back and laughed. "Now let us see if he remains interested in you."

Gavenia lifted her head; her gaze darted to the open doorway. Her pulse beat wildly as blood pounded in her ears.

She had one chance.

Pushing to her feet, Gavenia goaded, "He will never love you. You will always be a servant to him." Gavenia didn't know who they talked about, but by the reaction of Coira's heated face, she must have hit the mark.

Raising the dagger above her head, Coira screamed with rage, but Gavenia rammed her head into her stomach, knocking the wind from her rival. Coira fell to the floor and gasped for air while Gavenia ran out of the dungeon. She forced herself to slow her pace down the steep stairwell or risk losing her balance.

A scream echoed down the stairwell and Gavenia stopped. Coira would be coming down any moment. She hurried her steps until she found a guard racing up. Without pause, she kicked his face. He rolled down the stairs and remained motionless at the bottom.

Gavenia continued her decent. When she reached the ground level, she stopped and kneeled beside the guard.

He was still breathing. Thank the Gods.

Rising, she ran outside into a wall of immovable flesh. She went to look at her masculine obstruction, but he swiftly bent and swung her over his shoulder. All she could see was his firm, round backside in black chassis tucked into leather boots.

She kicked her legs, hoping to unbalance her weight, but he held her tightly as if she weighed nothing more than a turkey.

"Put me down. I demand you release me at once!"

Her captor remained silent and trudged her weight up the staircase. Her breathing became increasingly difficult, each step taking her air away.

When they reached the top, she heard Coira screeched, "That witch attacked me!"

"Out!" commanded her captor. The fury in his voice made even Gavenia shake with fear.

Coira shuffled around them and gave Gavenia a scathing look before fleeing down the stairs.

At last, when her captor released his hold, Gavenia would be able to see his face. She heard the click of his fingers and suddenly her eyesight faded into blackness.

She could not see anything!

"Dear Goddess! What have you done?"

He swung her over his shoulder and stood her on her feet. Rubbing her eyes, she felt his presence move closer to her.

"Why are you doing this? Please, I pray you, let me go."

The dark threaten to overwhelm her as she blinked, striving to see the feeble light from the dungeon's small window. Gavenia sensed that he was a hand width away from her face. She could smell mint. It was not an unpleasant scent, but she trembled all the same.

"Please, at least release this bind, I can hardly breath."

She felt rather than heard him growl. Like a living snake, the bind turned icy cold and loosened, releasing her arms only to wrap around her waist. Gavenia sighed. She was not released from it, but at least the bind was no longer tight.

She stood still, unsure whether to thank her captor or reach out and claw his unknown face. Silence grew thick with tension and unanswered questions.

His presence filled the room and enveloped her senses. "Say something," she murmured, but received no response.

He was so close, too close.

"Say something!"

He ran his fingers through her short hair and Gavenia flinched at the tenderness of his touch.

A low voice rumbled in her ear. "Coira will be punished."

The dungeon filled with a chilly breeze and the door slammed shut.

Her eyesight gradually returned and she ran to the door. Grasping the handle she rattled the locked door and pounded her palms against the unrelenting wood.

"I want to go home!"

* * * * *

Coira lay naked on the silky furs in her master's bed, the whip draped across her breasts. The door opened and closed and she smiled. She had been waiting for him all afternoon. The bed curtains parted and Coira gave her most sensual pose.

"Lovely," said a whiny voice.

Coira rose. "Evan, what are you doing here, and where is Master?" Her nose wrinkled from the reek of the steward's old tunic.

Evan sat on the bed, his glassy eyes shined while his gaze roamed over her body. "He has sent me to banish you," he replied, and skimmed his dirty hand over her breasts.

She recoiled and slapped his hand away. "He would never…"

"Aye, he would."

The Celtic Witch and the Sorcerer 67

Evan grabbed her wrists and pulled her off the bed. "Ye must go quickly. Master will be vexed to see you here." He threw one of the furs over her shoulder.

"Wait! I do not wish to leave. Where would I go?" Coira pulled the fur tighter around her shoulders. "I will not return to my father's vile farm. I would rather die."

Evan's gaze had not moved from the outline of her breasts and Coira smiled with a new ploy.

"Can I not stay with you in the village?" She dropped the fur around her shoulders to expose her breasts. His eyes brightened. Without missing the opportunity, he groped them. She moaned, pretending to like his careless attention.

Evan licked his cracked mouth. "Ye know that I also like men's flesh?"

"Aye." Coira rubbed his large cock through his stained kilt. "I can help lure them to yer bedside."

"Aye?" Evan showed his rotten teeth through a smirk. His hand ran down her stomach to between her thighs. His fingers roughly pushed inside her flesh. "Ye must remain out of sight of the master."

Coira nodded and suppressed a grimace. She turned around and bent over, exposing her buttocks. From behind, she heard him moan with delight and then fumbled with his kilt.

As long as she was within the fortress, she would have her revenge.

* * * * *

Tremayne leaned against the large table in his alchemist chamber. This was his personal room and was not entered by anyone but him. It held all his mother's magick books, potions, and ritual possessions touched by dark elements. Only a true sorcerer could use the power of his mother's mystical belongings. He enjoyed dallying in the dark arts, but grew weary over the years. Unlike his mother, the dark side did not corrupt his soul. Aye, he needed sexual energy for his powers to survive. But growing old was something he did not mind, in truth, it was something he strived for. However, with only seven moons left to Samhain, there was only one book that kept his interest.

He opened the ancient book of *Dark Magick*. The aged paper smelled musty when he flipped each one. Some pages were filled with spells while others held symbols. Only a witch needed words to chant a spell, whereas a sorcerer could use words or a vision. With a nod or a flick of his hand, he could create anything or punish anyone as long as they were in his line of sight.

With a relieved sigh, he found what he was searching for. Memorizing the symbols, he shut the book and replaced it in the dusty bookshelves.

"Soon, Mother, with the blood of Lady Gavenia, you will be released from death, and I will finally know the name of my father."

He settled into an oversized chair behind the table and stared into the flame of a candle. As a lad, he had done the same thing in the tower chamber while wondering who his father was and why he did not come to liberate him. The same chamber that held Lady Gavenia, held him prisoner but with more luxuries. Everything gold could buy, he had in his room.

Everything but freedom.

His only link to the outside world was the small window and his servant, Evan. Evan taught him how to read and scribe, and then gave him books on the dark arts. Once a year, his mother would visit. The very sight of him pained her, but he knew not why. Tremayne figured she was curious to see how his looks fared with age. She never touched him and rarely spoke to him, except to say he was cursed. Then she would leave.

It was not until he was eight winters, when Evan came to release him with the message that his mother was murdered by the Roberts clan and he was now Chieftain, Laird of the Campbells.

Tremayne shuddered at the memory, of the confusion, and lack of remorse for his mother, but mostly, for the knowledge she took with her. The knowledge of his father's name and of the mysterious curse he lived under.

His senses were jolted awake by light sobbing. He looked around his chamber, but it was empty. He rose and walked around the table and opened the door. The hallway was deserted, but the sobs continued.

"Who is there?"

His heart began to clench with an overwhelming feeling of hopelessness. Even his stomach felt raw with emotion. But it was not his emotion. Who was sending him this energy, this... feeling?

Tremayne took a deep breath and shook his head, but still the sound resonated within his soul. He could not shake the feelings.

Lifting the candle scone, he said to the flame, "Show me the wench that sends me this hex."

A ball of green light materialized from the fire and showed a vision of Lady Gavenia crying on her bed, her hair short like a man's. "This is impossible. She canna conjure her powers without being tortured by the tether. How is it I share her feelings?"

The emotion of despair caused havoc within his conscience. He knew what it felt like to be in that tower.

Nae! He would not soften toward her.

He would not!

* * * * *

Gavenia finally fell asleep on the uncomfortable bed. Curled into a ball, she had no cover to warm her cool skin. Her dreams consisted of running from a faceless demon, but no matter how far she ran, she could not escape. Just when the demon was about to grab her, she was taken to another dream, another place of serenity.

Her lover stood before her. With raven hair, his high cheekbones accented his square jaw line. While his muscled body was lean, he was not as tall as her father, although he towered over her. The black garb he wore gave him a sense of mystery, of danger. Gavenia smiled. She was glad he came to her this eve. She needed him. Needed to be loved by him.

He gathered her into his arms and lay beside her, face to face.

"My hair…" she sobbed and touched the short ends.

"'Tis beautiful," he said, his tender voice caressing her body like warm milk.

He nuzzled her hair and kissed her neck. A delicious energy skimmed down her back. "I do not want to wake up," she said, and closed her eyes.

"Then don't."

Suddenly, the cord around her waist unwound itself and flew to the corner of the chamber.

"I will chase away your tears, your fears." Her lover gently kissed her forehead and both eyelids. "You need not be lonely this eve." He then brushed a kiss across her cheeks and nose.

Her body became languid with wanting. His sweet breath was familiar, but she had never remembered the sense of smell in her dreams before. It mattered not. He was here and his body was exhilarating beside her. She looked into his dark eyes and ached for him to kiss her. To taste his mouth, his essence.

She pursed her lips.

Her handsome lover bit his lip and smiled with a glint in his eyes. Annoyingly, he lingered, and then kissed her with a hunger that belied his outward restraint.

His tongue danced with hers in a fiery possession. He grasped her body closer to his and wrapped his leg around hers, pressing his erect member against her upper thigh.

His clothes and her riding gown disappeared, leaving her skin naked against his. Dear Goddess, she loved this dream. Willing it to never end, she shifted on her side, positioning his manhood to rub against her sensitive flesh.

Her head felt light, beads of sweat dripping down her face. Her body was on fire and she wanted more, more of him. He cupped her breasts and she arched into his palm. They kissed hard and touched, grabbed and melded into one another.

Her pulse beat as wildly as her heart, her lungs burned for air. In frenzy, she rose to straddle him, his glorious manhood protruded between her legs. She gathered his erection and ran her hand up and down the length, enjoying the control she had over him.

He closed his eyes and groaned. The low tone sent new spirals of desire through her. She leaned over him and covered his mouth with hers while guiding his manhood to the outside of her entrance.

His lips brushed against hers as he spoke, "Are you sure you want to do this?"

"Aye, I really want to do this."

He waved his hand in front of her face and a burst of warm energy increased her ardor. Kissing him again, she pushed his tip inside her. With a gentle movement, she lowered herself until he filled all of her. Rising up, she took a deep breath. Having him inside was the most erotic feeling she had ever felt. Like having two souls merge as one in a powerful explosion of sexual energy.

She moaned with complete surrender.

What happened if she moved a little this way? Oh…that felt so good.

Circling her hips, she ground against him, exploring the exquisite sensations.

He sat up with her in his lap and she wrapped her legs around him. Gavenia raised her eyebrows, curious to the new position.

"I missed your lips," he offered by way of explanation and captured her mouth once more. The taste of his tongue and the feel of his slick body rubbing against her breasts drove her senses over the peak. Her base cravings urged her to rock harder against him.

Hurdled to a height of passion, hot blood raged through her body.

This was it.

This was it!

Aye, push into me harder.

Harder!

He gave a low, possessive growl, male and primitive. Grasping her hips, his body jerked. Thrusting further into her, he spilled his warm seed.

Her arms wrapped tightly around his back and she kissed his neck, tasting the delicious salt of his skin. Gavenia was glad this was just a dream, or else she would panic about falling with child. But she mustn't think of that now. She had her lover in her arms and never felt so feminine in all her life.

Still holding her, he lay back with her on top of him.

Gavenia repositioned herself to his side and he pulled her into the crook of his shoulder, resting her head upon his chest. They lay together, their breathing labored as one.

Lifting her hand, he pressed a kiss onto her palm. "Your energy is so pure. I have never felt so…"

Energy?

"What did you say?" Gavenia propped up on one elbow. How odd that he would talk about energy. Most people knew not of its existence.

He frowned and rose from the bed, their clothes appearing on their bodies once more. He ran his hand distractedly through his hair and began to fade.

"Please, do not leave."

His image returned and he leaned down to kiss her on the lips. "I pledge to return to you every eve until you no longer wish me too."

His silhouette faded into the darkness, leaving her feeling isolated, cold.

The moment she rested her head on the bed, she awoke to a ray of early morning light on the opposite wall. Gavenia's hands went to her waist. The orange chain remained in place.

Rising, she stretched her stiff muscles.

Curse that lumpy bed.

She used the cracked chamber pot and then stretched again. Besides her achy muscles, she felt revitalized.

Her stomach growled in protest and she clutched her abdomen. She had not eaten in days.

Gavenia heard several footsteps on the stairway before they arrived at her cell. The oak door pushed open to reveal three mute servants and two overgrown guards. They quickly gave her food and went about cleaning her dungeon, adding an extra chair with plush velvet lining. More servants entered with a large tub and began to pour buckets of steaming hot water.

Gavenia was stunned. Why was she being treated like royalty? As quickly as they appeared, the servants and guards left.

Ravenous, she ate the surprisingly delicious fare of rice potage with almond milk and sweet mince pies. Once her stomach was satisfied, she awkwardly undressed. The frustrating bind around her waist made it almost impossible to remove her emerald riding gown. Like a tight, icy girdle against her naked skin, the orange bind remained on as she sunk gratefully into the lukewarm water.

Leaning back, she wondered when her captor would show himself again. How long was she to wait? Even with the new furnishings, her imprisoned days would be tortuous. But the evenings...aye, the evenings would be filled with passion. Perhaps if she tried napping during the day, her lover would come all the sooner?

She hoped he would keep to his pledge and return to her dreams.

He must.

CHAPTER EIGHT

"I pray you, please tell me where she is," Adela pleaded.

Goddess Triana smiled as if Adela was an errant child who wanted a wooden hobby horse. The Goddess' flowing blue gown did not reach the floor, her face one of beauty and serenity. White hair framed her soft round face, accenting green eyes. Her spirit was one of calm while Adela's bordered on panic.

It had been six moons since Gavenia disappeared. She thought her daughter would have been ransomed and returned by now, but each day brought with it more anxiety.

"Do not interfere with her fate," Goddess Triana replied with a melodic voice. "No matter how painful."

The Goddess looked past Adela and through the window, her eyes unfocused. Adela looked behind her, but there was nothing but the view of the valley below. She turned, and the Goddess began to fade, a loving smile on her face.

"Please, wait!" Adela cried.

The chamber door slammed open and her husband stormed in. Oblivious, he walked right through the last vestiges of the Goddess' image. Not being of Celtic blood, he could not see the Goddess.

Phillip unsheathed his sword and threw it on the bed. With his fists clenched at his sides, he paced the floor of their chamber. "I have every mon scoring the countryside. I even sent a convoy to the main land, but so far all I have for my efforts is a small clearing with Gavenia's soiled clothes."

Adela shoulders lowered and her heart clenched with hopelessness. She collapsed on the bed, tears threatening her eyes. "I told you she could not be found."

Phillip sighed and walked over to her, opening his arms. Adela rested her head against his warm chest. The steady beat of his heart soothed her raw emotions.

"I tried a spell to conjure a vision of her, but something or someone is blocking my magick." Adela looked up at her husband's concerned face. "This does not bode well."

"There has only been one person with that kind of power," said Phillip, his eyes darkening.

"You don't think that Lady Torella is…"

"Alive?" Phillip finished her sentence. "Nae, it canna be possible. You killed her long ago."

"I heard rumors of a son, but none was ever confirmed." Her head jerked up. "Gavenia's vision."

"Pardon?"

"I conjured a spell to show who Gavenia's chosen one would be. The spell held a vision of a red boar with blood."

"A red boar lies upon the Campbell crest!"

"Dear Goddess."

"I will storm the Campbell's fortress and find our daughter."

"Nae, the Goddess warned me not to interfere. Yer life will be endangered if you go."

"If a Campbell has our daughter, then it will be their lives in danger." Phillip rose from the bed. Sheathing his sword, he bent and kissed her on the lips. "I will arrange the soldiers to return. By the eve of Samhain, my love, we will be ready to take the Campbells. Black magick or not, I will return our daughter to you."

"I want to come."

"Nae, it is too dangerous."

"I want to come."

"Your powers are weak on Samhain."

"And so will be Gavenia's. I must come." Adela stood and placed a hand on his chest. "If the Goddess is right and doom will befall my family, I want to be with my husband and children."

"I suppose if I refused, you would only follow."

She smiled weakly and nodded.

Sighing, Phillip kissed her lips. "We leave at dawn."

* * * * *

His boots' echoing upon the stone floor was the only sound Tremayne could hear while he paced the alchemy chamber. The night was still and unusually repressive for the time of year. He went to the square window slit, hoping for a cool breeze, but none was met. Crossing his arms, he leaned against the wall and stared outside. From the view, he could see the tower wall. Its impenetrable cold stone cradled the treasure within, the ravishing prisoner who waited for his visit into her dreams.

His body responded to the thought of her soft skin, full lips, and her open arms, eager to bring him closer. Not just into her body, but into her heart. Lady Gavenia made love with all of her soul. A soul, heart and body Tremayne yearned to possess. He found himself staying with his captive long after he had made love to her. They would talk till sunrise about their lives, family, and duty. He had to be careful not to tell her who he was, yet he suspected she held something from him.

Fear. Powerful and consuming.

He could smell it on her as well as hear it in her voice. Something kept her from her duty of marrying, even though she was filled with guilt.

It pleased him to hear it, even though he had no right to the thought.

He scowled and pushed away from the wall to sit at a long table with books and scrolls. He must harden himself against his emotions. His feelings–foreign as they may be – had to remain detached, cold. For on the morrow, he must spill Lady Gavenia's blood to resurrect his mother. If it was only for the sake of knowing his father's name, then he would not bring back his mother, but it was more.

Much more.

His mother would return to the living and Lady Gavenia would be sacrificed. He had no other choice.

Tremayne raised his gaze when a knock sounded. Rising, he strapped on his sword and opened the door. His steward stepped back in the hallway, his head lowered. Tremayne closed the door behind him. Evan knew better than to allow his gaze wonder inside the alchemy chamber.

Tremayne briskly walked down the hall, his steward fell in step beside him. "Is everything in preparation?"

"Aye, milord," Evan answered. "The ritual Celtic blade has been soaked with ox's blood and then cleansed with boiled mountain water."

"This pleases me."

"To think by morrow's eve, you will have yer mother alive and she'll tell you the name of yer father." Evan chuckled, his gaze shifting to Tremayne. "Your father could even be Laird Phillip Roberts."

Tremayne stopped and grabbed Evan's tunic. "What did you say?"

"Yer…yer mother seduced many men, one of which is yer prisoner's father."

"Lady Gavenia could be my sister?"

"Aye. Ironic is it not?" Evan peered closely at him, gauging his reaction. "Ye haven't bedded the wench, have you?"

Nae, it could not be. The thought tore at his insides. Releasing his steward, he stormed down the hallway. He needed to slay something...or someone.

Evan watched his master's stiff back retreat around a corner. Resting his hand on his sword belt, he whistled as he walked out of the dark castle and returned to his humble abode on the village outskirts.

A group of soldiers strode toward him, and he sidestepped to get out of their way. He cursed them under his breath. Things would be different once Lady Torella returned. She had a way of enchanting the soldiers to be more pliable to her whims. The men today were savages, rutting, disrespecting savages.

A heather-thatched cottage sat ridged in the glen. Evan preferred his abode to be away from the village's prying eyes and curious ears. The noises that came from his cottage were altogether unholy.

He opened the door, eager to see his woman in the position he left her in. Tied to the bed, Coira lay naked—her legs open, her breasts protruding upward. She slept peacefully, her chest rising and falling in rhythm. She used to resist being bound to the wall near the bed, the short chains allowing her to sleep and sit, but naught else. After a while, she came to accept that was how he enjoyed seeing her—enjoyed fucking her.

And fuck her, he did.

Often he would take his pleasure in her. Sometimes he would sink his cock into her while one of the stable lads would ram into his buttocks. Oh, the sensation of having both ass and cock stimulated. 'Twas truly remarkable.

He did not keep her tied up all the time. Nae, he was not a beast. She was free to go into the village to seduce a soldier into coming back to the cottage. A few soldiers were unsure of Evan, but Coira would kneel before them and play beneath their kilts, arousing them until they did not care that Evan watched and waited.

Artfully, Coira stirred the soldiers into frenzy, never allowing them release until Evan joined them. The soldiers were so aroused; they did not care where they stuck their staff, as long as it gave them pleasure.

Oh yea, Coira was skilled on how she guided their cocks from her mouth to his backside, all the while sucking and licking their balls. The same soldiers that looked at him with distain on the road would beg for him to spill his seed. The power was intoxicating and he owed it all to Coira.

His love. His woman.

Evan climbed onto the bed between her legs and took a big whiff of her glorious loins. He rolled his eyes and moaned. She still smelled from last eve's pleasure. Perhaps, the burly sentry's seed was still in her pink flesh.

Lowering his head, he began to lick her moist inner lips.

She slowly squirmed, but did not open her eyes. He darted his tongue in and out of her, lapping her warm juices into his mouth. A sweet moan escaped her lips and her thighs tightened around his ears. With her eagerness mounting, his shaft hardened against the bed, his balls becoming heavy.

He flicked her sensitive bud with his tongue and her body twitched. Her hips rocked to and fro, her insides pulsing. He loved it when she found her zenith. Any moment now, she would—

Coira's scream pierced his ears. Evan wondered how his master had any hearing left. Her body lay relaxed on the bed, her passion spent, but he enjoyed lapping up the rest of her juices.

The Celtic Witch and the Sorcerer   81

"Did you tell Master that Lady Gavenia could be his sister?"

Evan rose and wiped his mouth. "Aye, although it not be true. Lady Torella bed Laird Phillip after the master was born."

He kneeled on the bed and straddled her chest, his erection near her luscious lips. She grabbed the base of his flesh and licked the head.

"It matters not, old man. As long as he thinks of her as a sister, he will not fuck her."

Evan grabbed his staff and gently slapped her face with it. "Enough talk wench, suck me."

A smiled crossed her face, her eyes taking on a sultry look. Opening her lips wide, Evan pushed his flesh into the warm bliss of her mouth.

After Evan collapsed next to her and fell asleep, Coira lifted the key from Evan's kilt bag on the ground. Unlocking the chain, she rubbed her wrists and rose gingerly from the bed. Looking down at Evan, she grimaced. His crinkled face was relaxed and a loud snore came from his thin lips. She resisted the urge to spit on his ugly visage. The only reason she put up with his bumbling attempts at lovemaking was so she could stay close to the Laird. Well, truth be told, Evan was not that bad, but still, she did not like the man. There was something about him that repulsed her. Evan was not important, what was important was winning the master's attentions back. She just needed to get rid of that spoiled witch.

Why had the master not demand a ransom for milady? Why does he keep her around?

Ever since Lady Gavenia was imprisoned in the tower, her master had not been the same. While Evan thought her out seducing men, Coira would steal into the castle. She was careful to keep to the shadows, so the Laird would not see her, but the only time he came down to the Great Hall was to go to the tower. Other than that, no one saw him and no one from the castle made love to him. For a man with a huge sexual appetite, he could not possibly be satisfied with only one woman.

Could he?

Nae, the witch had enchanted him, made him obsessed with her wiles.

She must save her master from Lady Gavenia. Stop her evil ways from taking over his senses.

Coira chewed on her fingernails.

Turning away from the bed, she went to Evan's weapon chest and pulled out his crossbow and arrow. Bending the string, she tested the strength of the bow. Being from a farm, Coira knew how to hunt and kill an animal. This time, she would use those skills for a different type of animal.

She would kill Lady Gavenia and free her master from his obsession. He might even have Coira move back into the castle.

Giggling to herself, she dressed and left the cottage for the last time.

CHAPTER NINE

Unable to sleep, Tremayne walked up the tower stairs. He missed making love to her, even if it was in an illusion. What she saw as comfortable surroundings was a spell he conjured while they enjoyed each others bodies. Although women found his charms irresistible, it was in fact he who was under her spell.

Ironic really.

Daylight seemed to drag on forever. It was not until the moon was at its zenith, that she would sleep and he could visit her in the tower.

This eve was different.

He did not go.

Torn with the knowledge she could be kin, he had to keep himself away from her. How could he have these feeling for a sister?

'Twas impossible.

Nae, she was not his sister. He knew it with each breath he took. She was someone… special. Never had he felt a stir for another woman other than sexual pleasure.

When he thought about her…was with her…could smell her hair…well, he did not think straight. Could not complete a single duty without having her image invade his mind. Had this not been the case, he would have less cuts from training in the field with his men-at-arms.

Stale, musty air filled his lungs. He reached the top stair of the tower and halted to stare at his rough hands. The sun had yet to rise, leaving the eve as undisturbed as the prisoner behind the door.

He did not want to go inside, did not want to wake her from her dreams. From the illusion of him being her savior. Instead she would know he was not her liberator, but her enemy—the barbarian who would sacrifice her to free his mother from death.

Taking a deep breath, he opened the door with the key and entered her chilly cage like he had done so many eves before. Instead of enchanting her, he flicked his hand at the sleeping form. The orange chain gently unwound itself from around her waist. Like a glowing snake it slithered upon his open palm and curled into a tight ball. He closed his fist and it disappeared.

His mother told him the witch would be powerless on Samhain, and would be no threat to their ritual. Gavenia might as well be comfortable for her last day on earth.

He stepped closer to her bed. His chest was heavy with a sense of foreboding. She was breathtaking, sleeping peacefully on her back, soft, short golden hair fanned around her head, giving her an angelic appeal. Her light, long eyelashes rested on rosy cheeks while her full pink lips pressed together.

Was she disappointed he had not visited her dreams?

She certainly was not his sister. Gavenia was the complete opposite to him. Where her features were light and pure, his were dark and unholy.

She was good.

He was evil.

His whole being ached to touch her warm skin. To lie beside her soft body and cradle her in his arms. He must resist the temptation.

For when she woke, she would be more than disappointed, she would be furious.

Lady Gavenia would finally be introduced to Laird Tremayne Campbell.

Her captor.

Curse it all, he had to have one last kiss. One last taste of her mouth before she hated him. Sitting down beside her, he leaned over her to press his lips against hers. She moaned and he gently pushed his tongue into her mouth. The taste of her essence was more intoxicating than any spell he conjured. His heart yearned for more, but he knew she was close to waking. He had to stop. Had to pull away from her and never touch her again.

Gavenia opened her eyes and stretched her arms. Oh, he had come after all. She smiled. Her dream was so far filled with nightmares and blood. But now he was here, he would chase them away. She tilted her head a little, and wiped away the fuzziness in her eyes. Why was he standing above her and not in her bed? And why did he look somber? Had someone died?

She reached for him, but he stepped back.

Something was wrong.

She glanced around her dungeon.

Something was very wrong.

Confused, Gavenia sat up in her lumpy bed and looked at her fantasy lover.

Was…was she awake?

She couldn't be. Her lover stood before her in all his usual handsome glory. His black garb accentuated the hard muscles beneath. A body she knew intimately. However, his gaze was hard as he stared at her. She rubbed her eyes and swung her feet onto the cold stone floor. The chill crept up her legs and rested in her stomach.

She was awake!

Her lover was real!

Fear gripped her and she scrambled out of bed and backed against the far wall. "How is it you are here?"

Her dream lover cleared his throat, and for a fleeting moment, his blue eyes softened, then darkened once more. In a rich timbered voice, he replied, "I am the sorcerer, Laird Tremayne, Chieftain of the Campbells."

"Who...who are you?" The question seemed stupid to her, since he had introduced himself, but she did not know how he could be of flesh and blood.

Did he not kiss her moments ago?

"I am the reason you are imprisoned. This is my keep and you will be used in a ritual to free my mother from purgatory." He leaned causally against the wall, his arms crossed as if he were having a pleasant morning chat with an old friend.

"What ritual?" Gavenia asked incredulously. The wall behind her helped to keep her upright when her knees threatened to buckle.

The sorcerer pushed himself off the wall and stepped closer. "I did not mean for the dreams to go this far."

"Why? Why did you make love to me?"

Averting his gaze, the sorcerer turned his back on her. "I do not know." Opening the door, he called over his shoulder, "The ritual will take place this eve. Samhain's eve."

Gavenia jumped when the door slammed closed behind him. She was numb in her heart, her stomach churned with nausea. In one morn, her world crumbled further into darkness. The only slice of hope she had in this place was the same man who captured and imprisoned her. And now he wanted to kill her.

This was not the same man as her tender lover. It could not be.

She had to accept the truth—she allowed a man to make love to her and perhaps sire a babe. After spending her life avoiding men, she allowed her enemy to penetrate her defenses.

Aye...willingly allowed it.

Her legs gave out and she slid down the wall, tears streaming down her face. Sitting on the floor, she clutched her knees to her chest. Her skin was chilled and her muscles ached.

How long was she under his spell?

He had taken her maiden head!

He must have used his powers to take the pain away, because she did not feel her maiden head break. All she felt was desire and pleasure. Even now her body craved his love. His caress.

She slapped her face.

"Stop it!"

She would not love her enemy.

She had to stop acting like a spoiled bairn and toughen up. Even though the vision of her death was due to a birthing, it did not mean she could not be killed by dark magick. And what if she had fallen pregnant? In three seasons her vision would come true. Panic welled in her chest, burning her throat with fear.

Taking a deep breath, she tried to calm herself. She could not think on her death vision now. Instead, she had to focus on escaping. There had to be a way.

Rising from the floor, she touched her waist. The chain was no longer there. Her smile grew then faded. It was the morn of Samhain. The only day her powers did not work. She must think.

Around mid-morn, a guard came for her and led her downstairs. Perhaps this was the opportunity she was looking for. She must take note on her surroundings when she reached the outside. Surely, there would be a weak point in the battlements. Some feeble section in the Campbells defenses where she could escape.

An ugly guard with a wart on his cheek opened the tower door and pushed her outside. For the first time in many days, she enjoyed the sunshine on her skin.

The rising sun brightened the bailey and Gavenia squinted. The guard's hand pinched the skin under her arm and led her toward the castle. She scanned the area and found large battlements surrounded the grim castle and village. She judged the sentries on the wall and saw them raising a flag. The Campbell crest held the symbol of a red boar's head. Gavenia squinted again to focus on the familiar flag. Where had she seen that symbol before?

A sudden feeling of danger overwhelmed her senses. Intuitively, her muscle's tightened, her stomach clenched.

Her gaze swept the area.

Something was going to happen to her.

She heard a whizzing sound and feinted to the left. An arrow zoomed by her and landed into the guard's arm. He yelled in pain, and Gavenia turned to see Coira racing toward her, her eyes burning with hatred.

"Die witch!" she screamed, stopping to load another arrow into the bow.

There was no place to run without Coira shooting another arrow into her back, and her guard was on the ground, groaning in pain.

Terror like she had never known before coursed through her trembling body.

Dear Goddess, I am going to die! I am going to die!

Gavenia had only one chance.

Pivoting, she yanked the arrow out of the guard's arm and ran toward Coira. The surprised look on her face brought Gavenia precious moments before the crazed woman raised the loaded bow.

An eerie scream sounded and Gavenia realized it came from her own lips as she raised her bloody arrow and sunk it into Coira's chest.

Coira dropped her bow and fell to the ground, her eyelashes blinked rapidly and then slowed until they closed altogether.

Gavenia stood over her, speechless and numb. The only sound she could hear was her inner voice. *I killed her. I killed her.*

An older man ran over to Coira and fell to the ground. He cradled her lifeless body in his arms and sobbed.

Stumbling back, Gavenia could not stop trembling. She had never killed anyone before. She had not seen anyone die. Being sheltered behind Gleich Castle, her family kept her away from death. Until now…

Tears rolled down her cheeks. She wanted to go home. And cry into her mother's arms. She did not want to kill Coira. She did not want to kill anyone.

People gathered around and stared at Coira's corpse. The older man looked up at Gavenia with intense rage. He pushed to his feet and pulled out his sword.

She stepped back, bumping into the villagers. Would no one stand in to protect her from the man's wrath? She tried to run, but people blocked her way.

He was almost upon her.

She was trapped!

She squeezed her eyes shut, waiting for his sword to slice her head off.

Metal sparked against metal close to her ear, and Gavenia opened her eyes. The sorcerer held down the older man's sword with his own, and then punched him in the face. The other man staggered backward.

"Take yer leave, Evan!" the sorcerer growled, his eyes glaring with anger. The villagers took a step back in fear and Evan faltered. He lowered his eyes and returned to Coira's body.

The sorcerer turned to Gavenia and grabbed her wrist. "Ye make enemies faster than the English king."

Gavenia's face heated and her chest burned with fury. Yanking her wrist away from his hand, she retorted, "I did not ask to be here!"

He stood inches away from her, his chest rising and falling with heavy breaths. His blue eyes tried to stare her down, but she raised her chin and held his gaze. An uncomfortable silence descended between them, but Gavenia was not going to back down. Feeling anger was better than fear and remorse.

A slight smile crossed his lips and then disappeared. "Take her to my chambers," he ordered without breaking eye contact.

He then leaned in and kissed her nose.

Surprised, she blinked and shook her head.

Unnerved by the sudden change in the sorcerer, she watched him disappear into the crowd surrounding Coira.

Her arm was yanked to the left and she allowed a shorter guard to take her into the drafty castle. She followed him mindlessly. He could have led her straight into the large fireplace in the Great Hall, and she would not have noticed. Her jumbled thoughts held mixed emotions, her body, stupefied. What had happened to her this morn?

She found her dreams were real. She was no longer a maiden and could be pregnant. She would be sacrificed this eve for a lady she did not know. And she, herself, just killed the closest thing she ever had to a friend.

An uneven stone caused her to trip and kick her toe. "Ow." Gavenia bent to clutch her foot.

She could not handle any more!

The last vestiges of control began to slip. *Don't break down, do not break down.*

She took a deep breath and straightened herself. The guard looked at her strangely and opened a large chamber door. She held her head high and walked in with all the dignity she could muster.

This was *his* chamber. She knew it before she entered. The sorcerer's commanding presence was throughout the room. A large four-post oak bed dominated the chamber with a stately chair in the opposite corner. A wooden carved chest sat at the base of the bed while a wide table held several candles with ink quill and paper.

His chamber was clean and the rushes fresh, unlike the Great Hall downstairs. It was the one thing she did notice. The Campbell's castle was filthy. His house steward was obviously inadequate. Perhaps, if the sorcerer...

"Argh!" *Stop thinking about him.*

Gavenia twisted in a circle and landed on the bed in frustration. The fur coverlet cradled her weary body. Wrapping the pelt around her shoulders, she snuggled further into its warmth and his masculine scent enveloped her. She could not escape the way her heart skipped at the thought of him laying naked in the same spot she was in.

Why do I persist on thinking about him? Stop it! Stop it!

The door opened and she hastened to her feet. Her face felt warm from thoughts of him.

She must hate him.

Stay angry at him.

Aye, that was the best way. She could not see who came into the room, the bed curtains obstructing her view of the door, but she knew it was him. She could *feel* his presence enter the chamber. The sound of heavy boots came closer.

She balled her trembling hands into fists. She would not be afraid or allow herself anticipation.

The sound of boots stopped.

He was close.

Leaning to the side, she tilted her head. What was taking him so long? Was he waiting for her to come to him? She shifted from foot to foot. Waiting. It was agonizing.

Show yourself!

A hand emerged from around the corner of the bed. His palm held outwards, inviting her to take it. To accept him as her conqueror. Her master.

Nae! She must not. Her heart and body screamed to accept while her mind fought for control. He betrayed her and made her desire him. He was dangerous. He was her enemy.

While her mind flicked through all the reasons why he was no good, her quivering hand slowly reached for his. Her fingers glided across his warm palm. Her body heated with hope.

She was a fool.

He gently pulled her around the bedpost and held her hand to his chest while his other arm snaked around her waist. Curse his devil blue eyes and the black heart that beat beneath her hand. What was she doing? Her body melted to his hard contours. How could she not know this man was real and not a dream?

"Have you enchanted me?" she softly asked.

He smiled. "Nae, milady. Not this time."

"Then...then why do I feel this way?" Gavenia raised her chin, challenging him to explain. Dear Goddess, he smelled wonderful. Again, his breath held a slight scent of mint. It was familiar and soothing.

He did not answer and looked as puzzled as she did.

"I apologize for Coira," he said and released Gavenia. He turned toward a trestle upon the side table.

Without the warmth of his arm around her, a chill crept over her body, creating bumps upon her skin. Gavenia shook her head. "I do not understand any of this."

"Apparently, Coira was vexed with jealously."

"I did not want to..."

"I know." He handed her a goblet of red wine. "I saw from up here."

"You were watching me?" She took the wine from him, her gaze never leaving his.

"Aye."

He stood close to her. The masculine scent of his body enveloped her senses, causing her nipples to erect with expectation.

"Come, let us enjoy one another before we part." He sat on the bed and held out his hand. "I will give you pleasure like you have never had before."

"You mean, before you kill me," she said.

The words washed over her like highland snow. She stepped away. Her stomach turned with the knowledge this could be her last day on earth. It would be easy to succumb to his charms, his lovemaking. But she must not. Would not make love to the enemy, no matter how her body responded to his nearness.

A cheeky grin crossed his face, giving him a boyish appeal. "No woman has ever resisted me."

"I am not any woman." She sat in the hard chair and crossed her arms. "I am a Celtic witch."

The sorcerer pushed to his feet, his face sober. "So be it, milady." He opened the door. "I will have my personal guard escort you to the eve's repast."

Without a backward glance, he left.

Gavenia gripped the chair arms to stop herself from running after him.

* * * * *

The stars twinkled in the sky by the time the door unlocked and an elderly lady with gnarled hands shuffled in. She carried a satin ruby gown and slippers. After executing a curtsy, she smiled at Gavenia and laid the gown on the bed.

"Would you like me to dress you, milady?"

"Nae, 'twould not be necessary," Gavenia replied. "You may go."

"He has a heart."

"Pardon?"

"My laird. He has a heart," the old lady repeated. "He was treated poorly as a lad and it makes him guard his heart from others." She shuffled over to her and patted Gavenia's hand. "My dear child, it is there. You just need to be patient."

Gavenia did not know how to respond. She wanted to say, *"You crazy old woman. Yer laird is going to sacrifice me for his mother, but, aye, he has a heart?"*

Instead, she smiled and nodded. No point in arguing with his servant who obviously adored him.

After she left, Gavenia lifted the gown over her head, allowing the smooth material to skim along her skin. It was heavenly to have such a gown on her body. Especially one that was clean. The high-waist garment, with black embroidery along the trim, accented her curvaceous figure. She felt like a different woman.

Clutching the material, she raised the hem from the floor. The gown was a little too long and Gavenia wondered who owned if before her. It had to be someone taller than she.

She stood before the mirror and saw her mother's reflection. She never knew how much she looked like her mother. She wished she had a chance to say goodbye. To say she was sorry for not listening to her words of warning. Now it seemed it was too late. There was no escape for her. If this be her last night alive, then she was going to be honest with herself.

"How do you love and hate someone at the same time?"

CHAPTER TEN

With his pack of wolves following, Tremayne paced the castle's long halls all day. He tried to work in his alchemy chamber, but to no avail. His restless spirit would not be at peace. He could not go through with the ritual. A part of him always knew it would not happen. The moment he looked through his scrying bowl and saw Lady Gavenia dismount at the pond, his heart had been lost.

For certain, he was angry at first. Never had someone taken hold of his guarded emotions so completely. He thought if he captured the tempest beauty and took her to his bed, then he would no longer be affected by her. Did he not grow weary of all women sooner or later? But making love to her had the opposite effect. Instead of tiring of her, he craved her presence like a knight seeks honor.

How could he sacrifice her now? To part from her would surely tear his soul in two. And what of the consequences? His mother would not be happy. His father's name would be lost, and he would have failed.

Entering the Great Hall, Tremayne sat on the noble chair next to Evan at the high table and surveyed his hall for energy. Four couples were busy upon the ground in front of him while others talked loudly at the tables, waiting on food and ale.

"Finally, yer mother will return to us and this place will be filled with her power," Evan said, his words slurred from too much wine.

Tremayne cleared his throat. "I care not for her company, but for the name she would give me."

"Aye, once you have yer father's name, you can complete the ritual from the book of Dark Magick." Evan slurped another sip from his tankard. After belching, he added, "And that damn witch will get her punishment for killing my woman."

"Coira attacked first. Lady Gavenia had every right to defend herself." Tremayne growled. "Besides, I am having second thoughts."

"Sounds to me like you have been bewitched by the whore." Evan stared at him. "I suggest you squash such thoughts. We must begin the ritual, time grows short." The steward's eyes were blood-shot, vengeance shining beneath.

"I did not ask for advice and I know what is at stake."

Evan slammed the tankard on the table and rose to his feet. "Then kill the witch and be done with it!"

The hall became quiet and everyone looked at Tremayne. Their eager eyes glistened with anticipation to his reaction.

Tremayne calmly rose to his full height and stared down at his steward. Evan's face changed from rage to fear and he stumbled over his chair.

"I…I pray yer pardon, I spoke out of turn."

Tremayne flicked his hand and Evan flew against the wall. Arms pinned to his sides, the steward's clothes ripped from his body, exposing his flabby stomach and skinny arms. The Campbell clan erupted in laughter, pointing at Evan's discomfort.

A warm hand touched his arm and Tremayne jolted as if someone burned him. A soft voice spoke from behind. "Release him."

His gaze traveled the length of the delicate arm to see two pert breasts snug within the red satin gown. Her chest rose and fell evenly and her creamy neck held the face of an angel. More exquisite than ever, Lady Gavenia created a stir within his heart.

"Release him," she repeated.

Without taking his gaze from her, he flicked his hand again and Evan fell to the ground, his body clothed once more.

The hall fell silent. Not only had someone touched the wrathful sorcerer and still remained breathing, but gave him a command and he complied. If only his people knew how much power Lady Gavenia had over him. If only she knew. He indeed, would be in sorrow.

"Please, sit," he said, and pulled out a chair.

She regally sat and rested her hands in her lap.

The hall returned to its normal boisterous level. Some of the curious gaped at the sorcerer's honored prisoner.

Tremayne could not fault them. He, too, studied her carefully while her gaze roamed the chamber. Her stunning blue eyes widened at the rutting couples on the ground. He could not help but smile when her adorable face flushed.

"Why do you have people mating in yer hall?"

"I use their sexual energy."

"Have you no power without this energy?"

He knew she was asking for information. Perhaps, a chink in his armor? He found himself replying with honesty. "Aye. Without sexual energy, I grow weak."

She looked like she wanted to say something, but did not.

Tremayne placed his hand on hers. "Ask me."

"Did I give you sexual energy?"

He knew that would be her question. "You gave me more energy in one eve than a hundred women."

A slight smile tilted the corners of her lips as her gaze continued to travel around the Great Hall. One of his wolves nudged her leg and she absently patted behind his ear. Most of his people stayed away from the fierce animals, but she caressed the beast as if it were a kitten.

The serving maid placed two chalices of ale between them along with a handful of mint leaves. Tremayne threw a leaf in his mouth and a few in his ale.

"That explains why yer kisses taste…"

"…delicious?"

"I was going to say minty."

"I like herb in my ale," he replied. Pleased that she would think well of his kisses. "Try some."

She picked up a few leaves and added them to her ale. Taking a sip, she moaned with appreciation.

Tremayne wanted to carry her upstairs to his chamber to see if he could elicit the same moan while making love. There would be time for that later, for now he must tell her about the ritual. He would not sacrifice her to save his mother.

"Milady, I wish to speak of…"

Her brows furrowed and her face paled.

He looked in the same direction as hers. She stared at the Campbell's crest on the wall. Her aura changed into a mirror of colors. Tremayne felt her emotions scattering. She mouthed something, but he could not make it out.

"What is amiss?" he asked and glanced at his crest, then back to her.

Upon the table, her hands trembled. "You are the chosen one!" she growled, her eyes flashing with anger and confusion.

"I am the what?"

The double doors slammed open and his sentry ran to the high table. "My laird, there is an army at the gates."

"Father!" Lady Gavenia breathed. A light of hope entered her eyes.

A loud bang echoed from across the village into the Great Hall.

"They have filled the moat and are using a trebuchet to penetrate our gate," his sentry informed. "What be yer orders, my laird."

"Take milady up to the solar and guard her well." He turned to Gavenia and touched her cheeks with both hands. "I… I…"

He did not know how to tell her how he felt. "Wait for me."

He kissed her quickly and ran toward the doors, shouting orders to his soldiers.

At his side, he grasped the long metal handle of the broadsword. The heavy blade glided out of the leather scabbard with ease.

"Prepare for battle!"

CHAPTER ELEVEN

If she was to escape, now was the time. She might not have her powers, but she could at least try to outmaneuver the vicious-looking guard behind her. Memory of the sorcerer's kiss lingered on her lips and she touched her mouth.

"Curse my traitorous lips," she mumbled. She would not wait for him like one of his pet wolves. No matter how much she loved him, her clan waged a war outside.

They were almost to the solar when she pretended to stub her toe. Bending over she cried in pain. The guard leaned over her to see her injury and she swung her fist back into his groin. He tumbled over in agony and Gavenia sidestepped him.

The deserted hallway gave her hope. She ran freely toward the narrow stairway. Just as she was about to descend, a crossbow appeared dangerously close to her face. She halted and stepped back as Evan followed her up to the last stair.

"I hope I did not thwart yer plans of escape," he said smoothly, his breath reeking of wine.

Gavenia continued backward. "If you let me go, you will live to see the morn."

Evan laughed. "It will be you who does not see the morn."

A low moan came from behind Gavenia and she quickly turned her head to see the guard slowly rise to his feet. He gave her a murderous glare and she sidled around him against the wall.

"Go inside the chamber," Evan ordered.

Unwilling to remain under the angry guard's scrutiny, she obeyed.

Rubbing the chill from her hands, she paced inside the luxurious solar. The laird's sitting room held a lavish tapestry covering one wall. The Campbell's crest mocked her ignorance to its symbol.

The red boar.

How could she miss an obvious sign from the vision?

At the doorway, Evan murmured something to the guard, gave her one last glare and then left her alone with the steward. Gavenia sighed; she didn't know who was worse to be with, Evan or the irate soldier.

A shattering crash vibrated outside the castle. Sounds of chaos filtered through the large arched windows that overlooked the bailey. Ignoring the steward, Gavenia leaned out the window. Beyond the village, the front gate was destroyed and hordes of Roberts' soldiers piled through the timber wreckage. Their green and black plaids glowed from fire scones held in one hand, long swords glistened in the other. In red tunics, the Campbell soldiers rushed to fight the intruders, the clash of swords echoed in the night air.

Gavenia edged further out the window to see if she could find her father and brother, but it was too dark to see their faces. She searched for the sorcerer, hoping his tall stature would make him easy to find, but it did not. There were too many soldiers on the roads. Her stomach knotted with anxiety. She did not want anything to happen to him or her family.

Her hair was yanked from behind and she stumbled backward. Gavenia turned, rubbing the sting in her scalp.

She gasped when she saw a red pentagram painted on the floor in the center of the chamber. From the metallic smell, it had to be drawn in blood.

Evan laughed, his eyes wide and fanatical. He rubbed his face with both hands and left a smudge of blood on both cheeks. He crooked a finger at her. "Now is the time you die witch!"

Gavenia tried to run around the blood-drawn symbol, but Evan blocked the doorway. In one swift movement, he back-handed her across the face and she fell into the pentagram.

Her cheek throbbed with pain and her eyes smarted with tears. She propped herself up on both hands.

This is not happening!
This is not happening!

Eerie feminine laughter vibrated around the chamber, causing Gavenia to shiver with dread.

A woman appeared out of thick black smoke. Her ebony hair was in contrast to her lily-white skin while her blue eyes were the same as the sorcerer's.

Gathering her courage, Gavenia pushed to her feet. "You must be the sorcerer's mother."

The stunning woman flinched at Gavenia's words.

With an imperial voice, she replied, "I am Lady Torella Campbell, Sorceress to the Devil."

Gavenia gulped. She did not know his mother *was* a sorceress. Many times her own mother had warned her about women of evil magick and how they hunt Celtic witches on Samhain's eve to steal their powers and burn them at the stake.

Lady Torella smirked. "I see yer aura darkened with fear and well it should. But do not be too sad, you can be comforted in knowing yer blood will help me to live again."

Gavenia stepped back, but an invisible force kept her in the pentagram. "Your...your son will not allow anything to happen to me," she blurted, hoping her false words sounded convincing.

"Not allow it?" Lady Torella laughed again and then hissed, "He will insist upon it!"

"Nae!"

"Aye. If he does not acquire the name of his father, he will die on the day of his twenty-fifth birth." Lady Torella rubbed her hands over her breasts and moaned. Her eyes turned black as she continued, "My son will not only die, but his soul will be tortured in hell for eternity." Her child-like giggle was disturbing. "The lad will pay for my sins."

"How would his father's name save his soul?" Gavenia asked, her voice trembling.

"The mortal's name is given in a blessing for the Gods. Having a human sire is redemption for my son's evil blood. The Gods accept his father's name and thus allow him to live. The universe is balanced and the Gods are pleased. And so on and so on..."

"And you will not give it to him unless he kills me," Gavenia added.

"You are a wise little witch. Pity you must die by the Celtic dagger. I would have liked to see you burn...but alas, one canna always get what one wants." She turned to Evan and nodded. "'Tis time. Let us start the ceremony."

* * * * *

The Roberts soldiers spread through the village like locusts. Tremayne's men bravely charged the invaders, but they were clearly unprepared for the surprise attack.

Tremayne's first instinct was to use his powers and slaughter the enemy. It would be easy enough. One wave of his hand and the Roberts clan would fall to their knees.

An honorable death, nae.

A quick and painless death, aye.

But he could not bring himself to do it. This was not any enemy. 'Twas Gavenia's clan and her beloved family ran amongst the invasion.

Running into the fray, he raised his sword. He would have to defend his keep the traditional way and pray to the Gods he did not come across one of her family members.

A moment later, his prayers went unanswered. A blond-haired soldier wearing the Roberts coat-of-arms on his surcoat and shield, headed straight for him. The resemblance to Gavenia was staggering. His golden hair and angelic round face was the masculine mirror image of his love. This had to be her older brother she affectionately spoke of many times.

Tremayne sized up his opponent; the brother's mouth was set in a grim line, his hand clutching his sword. He was tall and judging by his build, trained often.

Sounds of the battle raged around them, but Tremayne paid no heed.

The brother spoke, his voice filled with fury, "So the mysterious Campbell chieftain does exist. The spawn of Lady Torella."

Tremayne smiled and answered, "My existence is no secret. Perhaps yer messengers are old and feeble."

The brother lunged and Tremayne feigned to the right with a speed no human eye could follow. He watched his opponent run past, his expression filled with surprise.

"What be thy name?" Tremayne asked. "So I know what to put on yer gravestone."

The brother's eyes narrowed and his teeth gritted. "'Twill be yer name you son of a whore."

Tremayne laughed at the brother's frustration, yet appreciated the man's grit in continuing to fight. Surely, the brother knew he was no match against a sorcerer's power.

He lunged again and Tremayne defended his sword's blow. Again and again their swords clashed. Neither one tiring from the fight.

"Why did you take my sister?"

"She looked like she needed a mon to satisfy her."

"Argh!"

The brother slashed his sword through the air and Tremayne effortlessly defended himself from the deadly blade. Tremayne could not resist baiting the man. He was having so much fun. It had been long since he had a worthy adversary.

A familiar face flashed by his side and Tremayne pivoted to see the guard he assigned to Gavenia.

With only a short lapse in time, Tremayne turned to see the brother rush him. He twisted, but the brother's sword sliced past his ribs. A searing pain stabbed at his sides, but he absorbed the wound and remained upright to block the next parry.

No one had wounded him with a sword. He looked up from the blood stain on his tunic. Panting, the brother's smug smile broadened on his face.

Tremayne growled, "Take a rest, angel boy." With the click of his fingers, the brother's feet remained fixed to the ground. He tried to budge, but ended up falling over on his rump, his shield and sword clattering on the ground.

Tremayne chuckled and ran after Gavenia's guard. He found him fighting a common soldier. Loath to wait for the skirmish to be over, Tremayne used his powers to throw the Roberts soldier into the air, his body landing a few paces away.

His guard nodded. "Many thanks, my laird."

"Why are you here and not guarding Lady Gavenia?"

The soldier tilted his head with puzzlement. "I was told you wanted me down here to fight."

"Who told you that?"

"The steward."

"Evan!"

He rushed back to the bailey. Every step he took seemed too slow.

Tremayne should never have left her alone. What had he been thinking? It was almost midnight. He went to run up the stairs to the front castle doors when a flash came from the corner of his eyes. He turned to find the brother lunging toward him. Dodging the blade, he defended the next blow.

"How did you escape?"

The brother smiled. "Mayhaps you are not as powerful as you think."

"I do not have time for this," Tremayne replied and flicked his wrist again.

The brother flew through the air and landed against the stone wall.

Tremayne could see the brother's reckless orange aura was still strong. He would have a headache, but he will live. His sister on the other hand...

He ran up the rest of the stairs and entered the castle. By the devil, he hoped he was not too late.

* * * * *

Adela sensed her children's distress all at once. Her son was in pain and her daughter's fear gripped Adela's heart. Curse these Campbell soldiers that blocked her path to the castle. Panic filled the villagers as they pushed past her to escape the battle. A Campbell fell at her feet and she leaped sideways. Her husband twisted around to make sure she did not trip over his opponent. She gave him a lopsided smile; even in battle he cared for her comfort. Unfortunately, there was nothing he could do for the internal pain she perceived from her children.

"My lord husband, we must make haste," Adela called over the deafening noises from the fray.

"There are too many people."

A chill ran over her body. Adela looked up at the castle, above the turrets circled an ominous black shadow. "Dear Goddess, let it not be her."

Her arm was pulled to the right and she stumbled behind her husband toward a soldier on a black warhorse.

Phillip shouted, "We'll take the stallion and make our way through the crowd." He led her to a wall. "Stay here."

She nodded and watched her husband attack the Campbell on horseback. Phillip was at a disadvantage being on the ground, but no soldier could match his skill with the sword. Soon, the Campbell lost his grip on his blade, and her husband pulled him off the horse, knocking him unconscious.

He led the horse by its reins over to Adela. His two large hands lifted her on top, and then he swung up behind her. They clashed slowly through the battle. Some Campbells tried to stop them, but Phillip eliminated any who came near. They reached the bailey and saw Callum slumped against a wall, his head bleeding.

Adela slid off the horse and ran to her son, her heart thumping in her chest. "Callum, are you well?"

"Aye, I am seeing double, though. Is that normal?"

Phillip growled, "Who did this to you?"

"Lady Torella's son."

"Stay with Callum. I am going to find our daughter," Phillip ran toward the prisoner tower.

"Nae, she is not there," Adela shouted.

"How do you know?"

"I just do. She is in the castle. I can sense her." Adela pointed to top level. "She is very afraid, you must hurry."

He nodded and ran up the stairs to the front doors only to stop mid-step. "Adela!"

Five wolves advanced from the hall, their fangs bearing with ferocious growls. Phillip slowly stepped backward.

Adela ran to stand in front of Phillip and held her hand up. "We mean you no harm. In the name of the Fliodhas, Goddess of the woodlands, I command you to back away."

"What are you doing?" Phillip whispered.

"I know not," Adela answer from the side of her mouth, "but it seems to be working."

The wolves stopped growling and retreated a few steps.

"Who would keep wild beasts in the castle?" Phillip asked.

"A sorcerer. Evil is near, be careful my love and find our daughter."

He kissed her, sidled past the wolves and ran into the Great Hall.

Adela turned to find the Goddess Triana in full form materialize before her. The usually serene beauty appeared sad and shook her head. "You should have heeded my warning, my child. Now misfortune will befall yer family."

CHAPTER TWELVE

A tight knot formed in Gavenia's stomach when Lady Torella's spirit circled her like a cat waiting to pounce upon its prey. Her cool voice spoke an ancient language, invoking a mist from the pentagram. Its color was rich lavender, but unlike the fragrant flower, the smell it gave off was putrid, like rotten eggs. The mist climbed her legs and swirled around her body. Gavenia did not think she could handle the stench as it raised higher and higher toward her face. Holding her nose, her eyes watered from the smell. Was she to die from suffocation?

Once the mist completely surrounded her, her muscles began to burn until she could no longer feel them. Her body was paralyzed. To blink was a struggle. She must keep moving her body. She must fight the curse.

Lady Torella skipped around her, clapping her hands with glee. "We are almost there, little one." She turned her head toward the door. "And here comes my son to finish the ritual."

Gavenia waited for the familiar figure to fill the doorway. Her only salvation. Her only hope.

Despite her fear, her heart skipped a beat when the sorcerer entered the chamber. What took him so long? Why was he moving so slowly?

"I am not too late, am I?" he asked his mother while training his sober gaze on Gavenia.

"Nae, you are just in time." She turned to Evan who remained quiet in the corner shadows. "Give my son the dagger."

Evan peeled away from the darkness and presented the dagger to the sorcerer, then stepped back against the wall. He smirked at Gavenia, his eyes glistening with an ominous anticipation.

The sorcerer's face was void of emotion when he grasped the dagger into his fist and held it low at his side. He turned to his mother. "What be my father's name?"

"I will tell you after you sacrifice the witch."

He shrugged his shoulders and stepped closer to the pentagram. "Very well, then."

Her panic increased when his eyes swirled with darkness like his mothers. She was looking into the purest of evil. A side she had never seen.

Gavenia opened her mouth and went to scream, but only a whisper came out. "Nae, my laird, you canna do this. You are the chosen one," Gavenia pleaded.

Lady Torella laughed. "My son, the devil's sorcerer, is the chosen one." She glided over to Tremayne and ran her finger down his jaw line. "How ironic."

He faltered, his eyes returned back to blue and his face softened.

Lady Torella commanded, "Kill her and let us be done with the ruckus outside. I ache to avenge my death on the witch's mother." The sorceress walked to the window. "I feel Adela is near."

The sorcerer stood still, looking at Gavenia. His eyes pleaded for her understanding.

"Kill her! Kill her!" Lady Torella yelled. "Or be condemned for eternity!"

"Nae," he replied. "I will not do it." The dagger dropped from his hands and clattered on the stone floor. "Release her, mother!"

"You fool," she snarled and ran over to him. Without warning, she slapped him and knocked him clear to the other wall. "Evan, take this dagger and kill the witch. I canna enter the pentagram."

Evan skulked forward and reached for the dagger.

"Nae," Gavenia screamed in her head, her voice cracked into a whimper.

"This is for my woman you killed, witch. She will be—"

"Stop this chatter and kill her!" Lady Torella ordered.

All Gavenia could do was watch as he entered the pentagram with the dagger held high in the air. Curse her muscles for not moving, making her vulnerable.

Her gaze was pulled to the sorcerer, pushing himself up from the floor. Evan saw her gaze shift and turned to find the sorcerer leap into the pentagram. They struggled for the dagger, the mist making them weak.

Lady Torella shook her head with disgust. "Men are so incompetent." She waved her hand and her son flew to the wall again. The sorcerer regained his senses and went to use his powers when his mother bound him to the wall with an invisible force. "Stay still, son, or I will be forced to send you to hell before schedule."

"Do it," he taunted, "just let her go!"

"My, my, we are chivalrous. You are a disgrace to yer heritage," Lady Torella said. "Evan, finish yer duty."

Gavenia's gaze traveled to the left toward the steward, his weary arm lifted above his head, the mist paralyzing his muscles. With a weak hand in slow motion, the dagger entered her shoulder. A piercing pain ripped through her arm.

He pulled the dagger out and collapsed to the floor.

Gavenia screamed in her head, her wound oozed freely from her arm. Blood, as red as her gown, made a trail down her hand and dropped onto the pentagram. A flash of purple light shone from the symbol and entered the sorceress. At the same moment, the mist disappeared and Gavenia was released. She collapsed next to the steward and breathed large gulps of fresh air.

Lady Torella squealed with delight as her body filled into flesh and blood, her cheeks changed in color from pale to a rosy pink. She was alive, young and beautiful.

The sorcerer was also released. He ran to Gavenia and kneeled by her side. Gathering her into his arms, he put his hand on her wound to stop the blood flow.

"Please forgive me," he said. "I should never have taken you."

Gavenia stared up into his eyes, they were clear and tender. "I am glad you did, otherwise, I never would have met my chosen one." She swallowed the lump in her throat, her shoulder searing with sharp pain.

He lowered his head and kissed her lightly, giving her strength when she had none.

"Come, I will see to yer wounds." He went to rise.

"Leave her in the pentagram, son," Lady Torella sneered. "I will need all her blood."

"Nae! You are alive. She does not need to die."

Lady Torella entered the pentagram, her powers seeming to increase by the moment. Her black eyes swirled with anger.

"Do not presume to command me. I have more power than you can imagine and I will see to it that you'll die a painful death." She loomed over them, her size becoming larger and larger.

A whizzing sound came from behind, and Lady Torella swiveled around to catch an arrow before it entered her chest. She laughed and broke it in half. "It has been a long time, Laird Phillip."

"Release my daughter or die!" he commanded, training his crossbow at Lady Torella.

"Father!" Gavenia called.

"Enough of these diversions." Lady Torella held out her hand and the Celtic dagger materialized. In one swift movement, she twisted to sink the dagger into Gavenia's chest, but Tremayne dove across her body and took the impact. His lifeless bulk landed across her lap.

Nae, he cannot be dead!

Her father charged Lady Torella with his sword. She straightened and waved her hand.

Phillip's sword was ripped from his hands. The claymore flew through the air and clattered on the stone floor, his body stood still as if paralyzed by lightening.

Lady Torella glared at Gavenia's father, her lips thinned. She stalked toward him and circled him like a predator.

"I have someone who wishes to meet you," Lady Torella said.

Her father gazed at Gavenia, his eyes full of dread and frustration.

Standing behind him, Lady Torella slammed both her hands on top of Phillip's shoulders and the air crackled with tense energy.

"Gavenia, I am sorry…" Her father's words faded as his body disappeared.

"Bring him back," Gavenia cried.

"Laird Phillip will never be found and can never escape. Your father might as well be dead."

"Nae!"

Lady Torella glided toward her and Gavenia tightened her hold on Tremayne. The gritty smell of his blood threatened to overwhelm her stomach, but she cradled his lifeless body, protecting him from his mother.

"All these interruptions," Lady Torella said with annoyance. She bent and touched her son's limp body and then they both disappeared.

Gavenia's hands fell through the air. Tremayne had gone along with her father and it was all her fault. If she had not left Gleich Castle, this would not have happened.

With blood stains on her gown and hands, Gavenia's wrenching sobs filled the chamber.

Footsteps sounded near the doorway and she looked up to see the horror on her mother's face. Fighting the rising nausea, Gavenia pushed herself to a standing position and then everything went blessedly black.

CHAPTER THIRTEEN

A candle glowed in the wall scone above Tremayne's head. He squinted, his eye-sight becoming accustomed to the dark, empty room. Fully naked, he sat up from the small bed and pushed to his feet. Where was he? The last thing he remembered was his mother stabbing him in the back. Twisting, he looked over his shoulder. It did not feel as if he suffered from the dagger. But he did feel drained of power, his limbs weak. It had been a long time since he had sex and without the energy; his body was now more human than sorcerer.

He scanned the small chamber for his clothes, but there were none to be found. Opening the door, he looked down the hallway. Whoever lived in this house liked the shadows. He padded down the hallway to a staircase that led into a main chamber with a side kitchen.

The main chamber was deserted and quiet. The only noise came from a cauldron bubbling over the fireplace and a goose roasting on the spit. The smell of cooked meat created juices in Tremayne's mouth. He was so hungry. He grabbed the turnspit and went to peel the goose off the metal pike when a voice called from behind, "Take yer hands off that!"

He pivoted to see a woman in a simple gray kirtle come through the door with a stock of wood under one arm and a long, slender stick in another.

"I beg yer pardon, mistress. I am in need of yer fare."

Without looking him in the eye, the bonny maiden with fiery red braids dumped the wood near his feet and the pulled a chair out from the small scarred table. "Please sit and I will feed you. That is why you are here after all."

"Ah, perhaps I could clothe myself first," Tremayne stated, curious to see a woman who did not at least blush at the sight of his nakedness.

She stumbled backward and bumped into the kitchen wall. "I...I did not know." Turning, she fled the chamber.

Tremayne looked down at his body. It was still hard and toned from days spent in the training field. Surely, he was not that ugly to scare a maiden so. He was used to women clawing at his body, not running from it.

The door to the adjoining room opened and the maiden returned with new clothes. She walked up to him without looking into his eyes and handed him a rough worn tunic and breeches. "These are all I have. Yer other clothes were ruined with blood."

He donned the clothes and sat. Silently, he watched the maiden gracefully move around the kitchen. She had a wholesome beauty, but was nothing compared to Gavenia. His chest ached with memories of her. Once he filled his stomach, he would leave to find his love. If his mother did anything to harm her...

He clenched his fist on the table. First he had to discover where he was and how he got here. "Pray tell, mistress, where am I?"

"Ye are on the edge of the dark forest, twenty leagues north of Dundee."

"Dundee? How did I travel so far east?"

The Celtic Witch and the Sorcerer

The maiden lowered her eyes and turned her back to stir the stew in her cauldron. "Are you of the Duncan clan?" he asked.

She did not answer.

"Perhaps you can tell me if you saw my mother. She is…"

"Aye." The maiden placed a pewter bowl next to him on the table. "She paid me to take care of you."

"I thank you for yer assistance, but I must hasten my departure. If you have a horse I can borrow until…"

"Sorry." She shook her head.

"You have no steed?"

"Nae, I have a horse, but you canna leave my lodgings."

Tremayne chuckled. "I hardly think you'll be able to stop me."

"She canna, but I can." Lady Torella strolled through the front door. Her black fur-lined coat billowed around her from the chilly breeze outside.

Tremayne stood up. "Mother, what did you do to Lady Gavenia?"

"Ugh, do not call me…Mother." She undid her gloves and threw them on the table. "Be content that I did not let you die."

"You were the one who stabbed me!"

"And whose fault is that?" she accused. "Now sit down and eat yer broth. I have news." She waved a dismissive hand at the maiden. "Alayne, leave us."

Once the maiden departed, his mother continued, "First, let me tell you, you will not be leaving here. I have enchanted Alayne's quaint cottage with a spell that not only keeps you imprisoned, but keeps yer powers obsolete."

Shock yielded quickly to fury. An angry retort remained lodged in his throat. "Why?"

"That brings me to my news. You are going to be a papa. The lovely Lady Gavenia is with child. Yer child.

Can you imagine the power of that baby? It would have good and evil magick in its blood. Why, the person who raised such a being would indeed be the most powerful in the world."

His mother's words blurred into one another.

Gavenia was with child?

How could he be so careless? Never had a woman become pregnant with his seed. He had always used a spell to prevent such an occurrence. She probably thought he was still dead. He must get to her. Somehow.

"Release me at once, Mother!"

"And have you seek the Celtic witch? Nae, I think not." She leaned toward him, her nose close to his. "That babe will be mine and I will not let anyone or anything stop me."

Tremayne swiftly grabbed her throat. "If you harm milady or her babe, I will…"

His mother chuckled and pushed him away, his strength was no more than a lad's.

"Do not be droll, my son. You will remain here until the day of yer twenty-fifth birth. Then you will die, yer soul paying my debt to the Gods." Grabbing her gloves, she rose and walked to the door.

"You had no intention of divulging my father's name," he accused.

"Of course not. Why do you think I kept you alive at birth? If it were up to me, I would have thrown you out the tower window the moment you came into the world." She opened the door and called over her shoulder. "Do not think about seducing Alayne into helping you. She is blind, so yer comely looks will not appeal to her."

Tremayne shot to his feet. "Where are you going?"

"To get married, of course."

* * * * *

"Curse this house!" Tremayne tried to leave through every door and window he could find, but his attempts were thwarted with a black energy bolt that burned his hands like a blacksmith's forge.

"When are you going to cease trying to escape?" Alayne nudged him aside and pulled closed the window shutters.

"Until I escape," he answered, and peered closely at her glazed eyes.

"Aye, I am blind," she said, her tone light. "I can discern shadows, but not specific features."

He looked around the clean, spacious chamber. Its furnishings spoke of wealth, even if the thatched house was old and run down. "Do you live here alone?"

"Aye." Alayne walked into the open kitchen and sat at the table. "Come and eat."

Tremayne followed her and sat opposite to the mysterious servant. "Are you not afraid to be left alone with a man?"

"Aye, I am," she said matter-of-fact. "But I am more afraid of yer mother."

"What has she threatened you with if you do not keep me here?" Tremayne asked, picking up the bowl of stew, he sipped the cooled broth.

Alayne lowered her eyes. "I would rather not say."

Tremayne felt frustration knot in his stomach. He had to get to Gavenia. She needed him and in truth, he needed her. Never in his life had he needed anyone, but he knew he would not be able to survive without her sweet touch and gentle glances. His heart ached for her kiss, to hold her in his arms. If he could, he would tell her everything would be all right, as long as they were together, they would raise their babe to be a good witch, like its mother.

He took a deep breath and glanced at his long hands where his powers usually gathered. They were becoming colder and weaker as the day progressed. Without the lovely Celtic witch to give him sexual energy, his powers would diminish altogether. If he was to break free from his mother's curse and return to Gavenia, he would have to do something he did not want to do.

CHAPTER FOURTEEN

The heavy bed curtains were shoved aside, allowing bright sunshine to sting Gavenia's eyelids. She covered the offending light with the back of her hand and groaned.

"'Tis time to wake, milady," her brother's wife said. Lady Vika was sweet and pretty with thin, snow-colored hair and large sapphire eyes. Her soft hand patted Gavenia on the leg, urging her to wake.

"Nae, I wish to sleep." Gavenia turned away from the windows and pulled the thick coverlet over her head.

"Perchance I can entice you from yer cave for one of the cook's delectable delights."

Gavenia raised her head, the smell of cinnamon wafted from behind her. "Which one?"

"Fine cakes."

Gavenia raised her languid limbs to sit against the backrest. On damp days like this, everything ached, including the scar on her shoulder from where the blade entered during the ritual. "I do not know what I would do without you, Vika."

Giggling, her lovely sister laid the trencher of goodies on Gavenia's lap. "I dare say you would never get out of bed."

Gavenia nodded and placed a loving hand on her growing abdomen. The sharp, crisp scent of mint floated from her goblet.

"Thank you for adding the herbs to my ale."

"I do not know how you can stand the taste." Vika sat on the bed, her nose scrunched distastefully.

Thoughts of her sorcerer weighed heavily on her heart. Why did his mother take his body away? Gavenia sighed. The question bothered her for two seasons. Her shoulders hunched forward. She did not get to tell him she loved him.

She mourned for two men—the sorcerer and her missing father.

She was the cause of their doom, and her body ached daily with debilitating guilt. But she must be strong. If not for her babe, then for her mother who had not left her chamber since their return.

With so much despair around them, perhaps her mother would have something to live for again. At least that was what Gavenia hoped. Who else would raise her babe when she was dead? If she was to have a boy, then her mother would be the last Celtic witch.

"Are you thinking of yer mother?" Vika asked.

Once again, Gavenia was astonished how Callum's new wife could read her mind. "Aye."

"Perhaps you should tell her yer secret." Vika's round, blue eyes held compassion.

"She does not need any more sorrow, besides, I only confided in you so you can make preparations before the birth."

"Worry not, my sister. All will be ready for when the day comes." Vika smiled and gracefully lifted herself from the bed.

"How goes my brother? I have not seen much of him since the nuptials."

"He is as well as can be expected. I do so miss him when he leaves." Vika absently ran her hands up and down the bed post, her eyes wistful.

"My brother is fueled by duty and vengeance. He will not rest until our father and Lady Torella are found," Gavenia replied.

Images of her own love sacrificing himself to his mother's blade haunted her dreams. Suddenly, her food did not taste appetizing. She pushed the trencher away. Her stomach turned with nausea while an emotional lump gathered in her throat.

Unconscious tears ran down her cheeks. It was a regular occurrence. Sometimes her heart cried even though her soul was numb. All of a sudden, her head felt too heavy and she fell onto the pillow to weep. Gavenia heard the door quietly close. Her sister had left. Silently, she thanked her. It was best that she was left to her emotions.

If truth be told, she did not want to be alone. Not really. She yearned for her sorcerer. Her lover. But he would never come to her again. Not even in her dreams.

Perhaps in the afterlife they would meet, and there, they would have a chance at love.

* * * * *

Even in his weakened state; Tremayne could sense Gavenia's sorrow. Two frustrating seasons had come and gone while he remained trapped within Alayne's abode. He tried to seduce, coerce, manipulate, bribe and even threaten the maiden into giving him sexual energy, but she would not submit. His mother's wrath terrified her more than his own, or perhaps, she felt his heart was not in the seduction. Indeed it was not. He did not desire any woman but Gavenia. But to escape, he needed his powers to break the curse upon the house. He had to give and receive pleasure.

Tremayne hoisted himself from the bed and changed into fresh clothes. The day of his twenty-fifth birth drew near along with his babe's delivery. He had to return to

Gavenia and protect their child from his mother. Time was his greatest adversary.

He found Alayne humming in the kitchen, her backside swaying to a popular minstrel's tune he had heard only at banquets given by Scottish nobles. Again he wondered which clan she hailed from.

Alayne turned her head at the sound of his footsteps and smiled. "The hens were busy last eve. We have a large batch of eggs. I think I will…"

Standing behind her, Tremayne touched her hand. "Let us sit. I wish to talk."

She faced him, her gaze unfocused. "I will not make love to you."

"What keeps you from my caress? Is it that you are afraid of a man's touch or that I will take yer maidenhead?"

"Nae, I do not value my maidenhead as others would. I know a mon would never desire me enough to want to marry me," she said with certainty.

Tremayne went to argue, but she shook her head and touched his hand.

"Please do not disagree. It is so. No mon wants a blind wife. I have come to terms with that." She reached for his face and ran her hands along his cheeks. "Ye must be very handsome, and I do desire you. I just canna…"

"I will protect you from my mother, this I promise."

She pulled her hands away from his face and lowered her head. "Lady Torella has…"

The door opened and they both turned toward the entrance.

"Lady Torella has what?"

Alayne leapt from her chair and it fell backwards with a loud thud. "Milady, I was…"

"I will deal with you later." Lady Torella glided into the kitchen. "Find me something to eat." Gracefully, she sat opposite Tremayne and seductively smiled. "I have an insatiable appetite."

"Have you seen Lady Gavenia?"

"I keep a close eye on her progress."

"How does she fare?" he asked, careful to keep his tone neutral.

She studied him closely and then replied, "She fares well, although, a little distraught. The lass has foreseen her death after the babe's delivery." His mother chuckled with amusement.

His temper flared with Torella's cruelty. "Pray tell, what is the jest?"

"It will not be the babe that kills her, but the black poison of Caerleon." She laughed harder. "Do you not see? She has resisted men all her life because she thought to produce a babe would be the last thing she did on earth. And then you came along and did the very thing she feared." His mother's face fell into seriousness. "Humorous, is it not? In her mind, yer love saved her, only to kill her." She took a sip from the goblet Alayne handed her. "No wonder she hates you."

"Enough!" Tremayne slammed his fist on the table.

His mother's goblet crashed on the floor near Alayne and she hurriedly bent over to wipe the spilled ale. An uncomfortable silence stretched between the three of them.

"Mother, I beg of you, do not harm Gavenia. You have given the Roberts enough pain. Please, leave them be."

His mother's smile did not reach her eyes. "They... killed... me!"

"And you have avenged yourself, now leave them be," his voice rose. "I pledge to you, that I will go to my death willingly if you let Lady Gavenia live and keep our babe."

"I see yer father's human blood has infected yer dark ancestry. You offend me with yer terms."

Tremayne shot up and leaned over the table. His voice deadly low, "Prepare yourself, Mother. This battle will not be surrendered."

A slight flicker of his mother's eyelids was the only indication he affected her. She stood, and the table flew across the chamber. Tremayne managed to step back in time before it took him with it.

Alayne screamed with surprise and backed into a corner.

"Do not worry, Alayne, she needs us to be alive."

Torella's red eyes narrowed. "I need you to be alive for the next two days. The lass is no longer of use to me."

Tremayne swiftly stood in front of Alayne, shielding her. "Goodbye, Mother."

She flinched. "Enjoy eternity in hell." Her laughter echoed around the kitchen long after she disappeared.

Tremayne sighed, tilted the kitchen table back on its legs and dragged it to where it belonged. He righted the chair at the table and sat. Resting his head in his hands, he growled with frustration.

"Is there a cure for the black poison?" a tentative voice came from behind.

"Aye, but the herbs are difficult to find and I would need to brew the potion," he mumbled, his voice defeated.

A soft hand lifted his head. Alayne's green eyes softened like the clear sea. "I will get the potion and take it to yer lady."

"Even if you found the ingredients, you could not travel across the country in time."

"We can try," she offered.

After a long pause, he kissed her on the cheek. "I hope you have a good sense of smell. You are going to need it to find these herbs."

Alayne gave him a reassuring smile. "My nose has never let me down."

The Celtic Witch and the Sorcerer 127

* * * * *

Drops of boiling water splattered on Tremayne's hand when he lifted the cauldron pot from the fireplace. He set the pot on the table and then went to Alayne's cupboard. Searching the well-stocked contents, he rubbed the hard stubble on his chin. "If only I had access to my alchemy chamber."

His fingers drummed on the cupboard door while he scanned the countless clay pots and fabric bags of herbs. "Aha!"

Balancing three pots of dried herbs in his arms, he set them on the table.

"Thyme, a protection from evil." He sprinkled the herb into the cauldron, then replaced the pot and picked up the next. "Three pinches of Juniper to repel dark spirits and…one dash of Valerian, to deflect evil plans from milady."

The wooden spoon swirled through the watery contents. He bent over the cauldron and sniffed the sweet-tangy aroma. There still was a lot missing.

"Where is Alayne?"

He glanced at the doorway. She had left that morning and dusk was now approaching. Alayne's fortitude reminded him of Gavenia. The very thought of his love heated his blood. He would do anything to be with her right now.

The front door opened and Alayne rushed through, her scarlet hair was messed with a twig in her braid. She emptied a sack of plants on the kitchen table.

"I was able to find all of the ingredients except the mint."

"That is all right, this potion will still work without it. She will not like the taste, but that will be the least of her worries." He looked at her and pulled the green stick from her hair. "What took you so long?" his tone held no reproach.

"I could not purchase all of them from the crone in the nearby village, so I searched the field near the river."

Blind or not, Alayne really was remarkable.

"Get some rest, lass. Unfortunately, this potion is going to take some time."

CHAPTER FIFTEEN

Sunrise filtered into the kitchen through cracks in the wooden shutters when Tremayne corked a vial of the final potion. He ran his hands down his face and collapsed onto the hard chair. The eve's precious moments were spent mixing and brewing, only to find he could not get the right consistency. After throwing out the contents three times, and cursing his mother in several different languages, fortune finally took pity on him. With the last of his ingredients, he had the potion.

His large boots thumped upon the stairs, his feet dragging with each step. The door to his room screeched open when he entered. He sat on the edge of the bed and pulled off his boots, each one landing with a loud thud on the floorboards.

Behind him the bed moved and groaned. His head turned sharply to see Alayne asleep in his bed, her slim shoulders exposed. The curve of her breasts peeked from beneath the coverlet. Was she waiting for him? He could not believe she changed her mind. Perhaps she had lost her way in the house. Tremayne shook her shoulders and Alayne slowly woke and smiled.

"Are you finished?" she asked, rubbing the sleep from her eyes.

"Aye, but it is no use. You will not be able to travel across country in time to save milady. I have failed."

Torment ate at him from inside. His head fell onto the bed, his back facing Alayne. Defeat was not something he could ever get used too, but to have Gavenia die at his mother's hands while he waited for his own death was agonizing.

Alayne ran her hands over his rigid shoulders. The contact sent energy through him, and his whole body stiffened. She tugged on his shoulder and pulled him down to lie on his back. "What are you doing?"

"I am giving you back yer powers."

"I…"

"Do not speak or else I will change my mind."

"Alayne…"

"Please. I could not live with myself, knowing I could have done something to save yer lady."

He didn't need to be offered twice. "I will be gentle," he assured and rose from the bed to undress. It was some time since he last lay with a woman, but he would force himself to go slow. Alayne deserved tenderness.

His manhood stood erect, and familiar stirrings of arousal increased the energy around his body. He was finally going to get his powers back. Tremayne sat on the bed beside Alayne and peeled away the covers. The early sunlight glowed upon her breasts, her nipples erect from the sudden chill.

Her hands fidgeted at her sides and Tremayne wished he had another way of regaining his powers. Taking a blind girl's maidenhead would never have bothered him before, but it did now.

Alayne must have sensed his trepidation, because she pulled the back of his neck down. Face to face.

"I want you to make love to me," she said and lifted her head to kiss him on the lips. "Ye may be the only mon who would ever touch me."

He breathed on his chilled hands to warm them before lightly running them over her taut nipples. A gasp came from Alayne. Her arousal gave him encouragement to continue.

"You have beautiful breasts, Alayne." His fingers tweaked each nipple, causing her breathing to increase. "Any mon would be lucky to touch you."

He lowered his head and flicked the hard buds with his tongue, his hands ran over her flat abdomen and down between her legs. Resisting the urge to touch her most sensitive spot, he massaged her inner thighs, allowing her to grow accustomed to the new sensation of having a man's hands upon her flesh.

Lapping her breast, he moved his body close to hers. Alayne's skin was warm against his, her hip pressed closer to his cock. The pressure sent a thrilling sensation through his body. He wanted to climb on top of her and sink it in her warm abyss, but he knew she was not ready. He grazed his hand over her sensitive mound and she arched closer to his fleeting touch. Aye, she was almost there. He allowed his fingers to brush across her mound again and she opened her legs wider, permitting him better access.

His middle finger glided easily between her moist lips. The silky feel of her arousal increased his desire. Lightly he circled her sensitive bud, around and around. He dipped inside her opening and the juices oozed around his finger. The warm walls of her body hugged his finger, urging him to explore further. His shaft pulsed, anticipating the same welcome his hand was receiving.

The stirrings of power flowed through his veins. He needed more to defeat the curse on the house, but he had enough to take away any pain Alayne would feel when he entered her for the first time.

With one last flick from his tongue on her nipple, he raised his hand and sucked her essence from his fingers. Alayne's eyes glistened with wanting.

She was ready.

Shifting his weight, he climbed on top of her, her legs cradled around his waist. With one hand, he waved it over her face. *Take away her pain.*

A violet light shot from his hands and surrounded Alayne's body. Only he could see the power he wielded. It felt good to be using magick again, even if it was a diminutive spell.

The aching head of his cock throbbed near her entrance. The slick heat rubbed against his tip. Devil's balls, she felt good.

"Are you sure?" he asked. He stared into her unfocused blue eyes and waited. His arms strained while he hovered over her. Sweat poured down his forehead and stung his eyes, but he was not going to plunge inside her until he got the word.

She nodded.

Good enough.

He slowly eased himself into the hot, sweet pleasure. The canal expanded, massaging his manhood. His body wanted to rock inside and out, fast. Increase the stimulation he had been denied for so long, but he resisted.

His attention was pulled back when stopped by Alayne's barrier. He pushed through her maidenhead, and studied her features. A smile whispered across her face while her chest rose and fell. She was in no pain. Alayne's red aura showed she was in the throes of passion. He kept a slow pace, rhythmic and sensual. Even though she was enjoying their love-making, he knew Alayne was holding back.

They must both reach their peak if he was to gain full powers.

Lowering himself, he whispered against her ear, "Release yer inhibitions, lass, and take me into yer body and soul."

She screamed.

Like an overflowed dam releasing its water, her hips ground against Tremayne, manipulating his shaft by her pulsing insides. She felt incredible! His body strained to stay on top of her, taking the onslaught of her frenzied hips.

Toward the end of her pleasure, he allowed his desires to explode, and he pushed inside her. The moment his seed was released, an inner sexual power shot through his body. An animalistic growl erupted from his chest.

Rising up, he threw his head back, his arms open wide. A glow of golden light surrounded his body.

His powers had returned!

A pain shot through his abdomen and he doubled over, clutching his stomach. "Ah!"

Alayne raised her head, concern etched on her face. "What is amiss?"

He rolled off her body and to the side. What was happening to him?

"Ah!"

"M'laird?"

"I...I know not." The pain seemed to subside, but left him feeling weak. "'Twas like a dagger slicing me from inside, out."

Alayne supported herself with one hand, her other hand rested on his chest. "It sounds like you were in a state of parturient."

"Of what?"

"What a woman feels when bearing a child."

Tremayne jolted up in bed. "Gavenia!"

CHAPTER SIXTEEN

"Argh!"

"Milady, are you well?" Vika asked her.

"The babe...it is coming." Gavenia clutched her stomach. Pain tore through her like she was being ripped apart.

Vika cradled her elbow and helped Gavenia up from the chair, the scenic tapestry dropped from her lap to the floor in the solar.

"'Tis wondrous news the babe is finally coming," Vika said.

Gavenia scowled at her sister. "It does not feel wondrous!"

Vika chuckled sweetly. "Soon the pain will be over and yer babe will grace the world with its magick."

They stumbled through the hallways together and Gavenia stopped her sister. "Vika, I am scared. I do not want to die."

Her sister patted her hand. "Perhaps yer vision was wrong, dear."

Gavenia shook her head and kept walking. "Nae, 'twas foreseen."

"Let us not think on it. You need to use all yer energy for birthing the child."

Thankfully, before the next spasm contorted her body, Gavenia arrived in her chamber and lay on her bed.

"Argh." She clutched her stomach and glanced up at her sister's concerned face. "All right, I do not wish to do this anymore."

Vika giggled and pulled the coverlet to Gavenia's chin.

"Could you request my mother's presence?" Gavenia grimaced through her teeth.

Vika nodded. "I will be right back."

In her white chamber gown, her mother rushed into the room. "Oh, my darling. The babe is coming." Adela sat on the bed and hugged Gavenia. "How do you feel?"

"Like two knights are jousting in my stomach."

Her mother's hand ran over her abdomen, poking and prodding Gavenia like she was a mare having a foal. "Mother!"

"By Jupiter, it will not be long. Darling, try to relax."

Gavenia screamed. The pain was getting worse; the air in her lungs seemed thinner. "Mother, I need to tell you something."

"I know. I am so sorry I have not been here for you. Yer father's disappearance has stolen my days. No matter how many spells I cast, I canna find him." Black lines under her mother's eyes showed how little sleep she had.

"Mother...I forgive you. But that...was not what I wanted to talk about."

"Do not worry. Yer birth lasted for three moons and I thought you would never come out, but you did in the end. Be patient."

"Nae, Mother. That is not..."

Vika hastened into the chamber. "I have extra cloths coming and hot water."

"Excellent," Adela said and rose to face Vika.

Their chatter grated on Gavenia while she huffed through the next spasm. When would this pain end? No one told her it was going to hurt this much. Surely, she would die before her babe came into the world. She had to be strong and not allow that to happen. She must stay alive long enough for her child to be born.

"Mother," she whispered, her throat raw from screaming.

Adela turned to face her. "Is there naught I can do for you?"

"Listen to me. Tell Callum, that I love him and I hope he finds Father."

"Gavenia, you can tell him yourself after yer strength returns."

"And," Gavenia continued, "I love you—I pray you do not hold any guilt over what is to come."

Adela sat by her side again and touched her shoulder. "Why do you say these things?"

Another pain sliced through her body and Gavenia growled, unable to scream anymore.

"Do not overexcite yourself," Vika said and wiped a wet cloth across Gavenia's face and mouth, briefly cutting off her air supply. She was having hard enough time breathing as it was.

Gavenia turned her head away. "Stop that, I canna breathe," she snapped and instantly regretted it. "I apologize, Vika, for my foul disposition."

"Daughter, you are having a babe, of course you are in a foul disposition." Her mother shifted sweat laden hair from her face.

"I must tell you something." Gavenia looked into her mother's troubled eyes.

Vika announced, "I do not think this is the right time…"

"There will be no other right time." Gavenia felt the stirrings of pain about to increase again. "Mother, my death vision..."

"Aye."

"When my babe is born." Gavenia swallowed. "I will die."

* * * * *

Impervious to his nakedness, Tremayne ran down the stairs, the steady patter of Alayne's bare feet following him.

He grabbed the potion from the table and placed the vial into Alayne's hand. "You must tie this around my neck after I transform into a falcon."

"I pray yer pardon?"

"I will transform into a bird so I can fly to Gleich Castle. That is our only hope."

Dread crossed Alayne's delicate features. Tremayne kissed her cheek and lifted her hand to the side. "Once I have turned, I will perch on yer arm. Loop the vial's string around my neck."

She nodded. Alayne looked like she wanted to speak, but did not utter a word.

Tremayne went to the door and opened it. Palms outwards, he chanted, "Unbind this house, three by three. By my powers, set me free."

He walked to the threshold and stuck his hand out the doorway. The cool morning breeze caressed his skin. At last, he was free! With only one day left to live, he would use it to save his fair lady.

"M' laird?"

"Aye."

"About yer mother..."

"Aye, you must leave this house and travel to Gleich Castle. If fortune is on our side, Lady Gavenia will protect ye, even if I cannot."

"But..." Alayne gazed at him in despair.

"What is amiss, lass?"

A sharp pain went through Tremayne, and he doubled over. How did women stand this torture? He had caused this to Gavenia. Guilt wracked his body along with the convulsion.

His powers could take away his pain, but he refused to consider the notion. The physical and emotional pain connected him to Gavenia. He would not be free from the torture, if she was not.

Alayne grabbed his arm and led him to a kitchen chair. He had no time for this interruption.

"Breathe through the pain," Alayne said, her calming tone soothing his nerves.

He took a deep breath and released it. The spasms subsided. He rose weakly to his feet. "I must away."

Alayne raised her hands to his face and cradled his jaw line. She kissed him on the lips and stepped back. "I wish you all success, Laird Tremayne Campbell."

"You have my undying gratitude, Mistress Alayne." He granted her a courtly bow.

Without further word, he transformed his body into a kestrel falcon. Brown and black feathered wings expanded in rapid beat, hovering. His eyesight increased to where he could see an ant crawl between the floorboards in the next room.

Alayne held out her arm and he landed softly on it, careful his claws did not rip her tender skin. She slipped the vial's string around his slender neck and kissed his beak.

"Take flight, my friend, and save yer love."

* * * * *

Vika edged toward the door, mother and daughter were talking in hushed tones, oblivious to her presence. "I...I'll go fetch ale for Lady Gavenia."

Closing the door behind her, Vika jumped when a young maid pulled up short before crashing into her.

The Celtic Witch and the Sorcerer 139

"I pray you pardon, milady," the maid curtsied. "I have mead for Lady Gavenia."

"I will take it in." Vika forced a smile and took the wooden pitcher from the lass's hands. "Ye may return to yer duties."

The maid bobbed a curtsey and left.

Vika looked into the liquid and swirled the contents within the pitcher. The aroma of mint wafted up to her nose and she grimaced. She turned and walked down the long hallway, then entered her chamber on the eastside of Gleich Castle. The room was small, but afforded her the morning light. Once the bolt was behind the door, she waved her hand over her face.

The dainty lady transformed into her usual sultry self. Torella smiled and glided further into the room. Betrothed to Laird Callum, the real Lady Vika gave her a perfect way into Gleich Castle. Too bad she had to die in order for Torella to copy her features.

She placed the pitcher on a table near the bed and ran her hands down the familiar curves of her voluptuous body. She missed her sensual form; although Lady Vika's petite shape did give her pleasure when Laird Callum visited her chamber in the early morn. Torella had never fucked a warlock before. She suspected the lad had no idea the underlining Celtic power he possessed. Just as well he could not access it.

But she could through sex.

Once his sister was dead, he would need someone to console him. Hmm, the mere thought of his hard cock filling her mouth aroused her powers.

Torella pulled a small vial out of the plain wooden chest she stole from Vika's carriage. Uncorking the lid, she chuckled beneath her breath. To think the handsome Laird Callum searched the country for the sinister sorceress, when she has been in his bed all along.

Ten drops of the black poison of Caerleon fell into the pitcher and Torella stirred the ale with her finger. By sunrise, she would have possession of the babe and her son would pay for her sins in hell.

It was splendid to be alive again.

Tremayne's words of battle echoed through the black stillness of her mind. She giggled at his bravado. What could he do from his enchanted prison? Ink a nasty scroll?

"I wonder how he is fairing on his last day on earth."

Out of a chest, she pulled a metallic scrying bowl adorned with emerald stones and Celtic symbols. She poured the rest of last eve's red wine from a goblet into the bowl. It was not much liquid, but it would do. The tart aroma wafted around her while she waved her hand over the potion.

"Show me what I want to see. Show me…my son."

The wine glistened on the surface, the ruby texture illuminating with light. A vision appeared of a falcon flying against the wind.

"A bird…"

She gasped.

"Tremayne!"

How did he escape?

Alayne.

Curse that blind whore! The wench would be dealt with later. For now, she would take care of Tremayne's untimely chivalry. Peering into the bowl, she said, "Lets see, my son, if you can fly without wings."

Torella clicked her fingers and laughed.

* * * * *

Tremayne was exhausted. He had flown most of the way with only a few breaks to rest. If he could only reach the glen near Gleich Castle, he would change into a stallion. Perhaps the extra muscles in his hind legs would give him more speed then these weak wings. He still had a lot of ground to cover before he could change to a land animal.

A bolt of black lightening flew across the sky toward him. This was not going to be good. Thump! The lightening hit his light-weight body and knocked him backwards.

Dear Gods!

Swiftly, he lowered his beak and dived for the ground, using his wings to balance the air. He had to land before he completely transformed into human. The black energy followed his descent, pulling and tugging at his limbs.

Nae, not yet!

His wings extended slowly into arms, his body filling out into torso and legs. His male body had completely transformed and he fell through the air with no resistance.

The tree tops moved faster toward him. Too fast.

The impact of his fall broke the branches of an old oak tree; his face and body were mercilessly scratched and battered, descending from one branch to another until he landed on his back with a thud on the ground.

He spat a leaf out of his mouth.

"Bitch!"

Pain coursed through his battered limbs, sweat stinging the open cuts upon his naked skin. He groaned, feeling like every bone in his body was broken.

His hand felt around his bare chest and neck. The vial! It was gone. The string must have broken on his fall down. Frantically, he scanned the area and found the bottle sticking out from beneath brown leaves.

Gingerly, he reached over and studied the container. At least it was not broken. With a lot of moans and cursing, he pushed himself upwards. Lifting his hand, he waved it over his naked body to heal the injuries.

Nothing.

He did it again.

No change.

She had completely stolen his powers.

"You could have at least left me with garments," he shouted to the sky.

With the sheer force of will, he struggled to get up. His twisted left ankle screamed with pain when he placed pressure upon his bare feet. He sighed with exhaustion and began to limp.

He had two leagues.

Two whole leagues to Gleich Castle.

He clutched his abdomen again. The spasms were coming closer in time. Gavenia's fear and anxiety was rising. He fell to his knees again. Damn these child bearing pains!

Must rise… and… keep going. He had to reach Gavenia. No curse, pain or sorceress would stop him. Nothing would stop him.

Well… almost nothing.

He looked up to find the tip of a sword pointing at his face. Recognition shot through his body.

As in much pain as he was, Tremayne could not resist taunting.

"Laird Callum, you look tired."

* * * * *

"'Twill not be long now," Gavenia's mother soothed, dabbing a cool cloth across her brow.

Gavenia's skin was hot and sticky from sweat; her muscles ached, draining her energy. Her mother talked of the baby coming, but her words felt more cryptic than comforting.

'Twill not be long before I die.

Memories of the death vision haunted her every day of her life. And now it would become her reality. She did wonder who the stranger was at the end of her vision—the mysterious man who burst into her chamber after she died. His face was never clear to her. She guessed she would never know.

The Celtic Witch and the Sorcerer 143

"Mother?"

"Aye."

"Do you think I will see my sorcerer when I die?"

Adela glanced away, but not before Gavenia recognized the hatred burning in her eyes.

"Mother, please do not think badly of him."

"I…I canna," Adela said and faced her, her eyes glistening. "Because of him, you were imprisoned and yer father was taken."

"Nae, he did not take Father."

"Aye, but we would not have been at his castle if not for…"

"I, too, share the blame." Gavenia's chest tightened.

"Nae! 'Twas not yer fault." Adela threw her arms around Gavenia.

Her abdomen tightened, the pain was coming. Gritting her teeth, she said, "Let us forgive…the…past."

She screamed.

Her mother grasped her hand, and Gavenia squeezed it.

The door opened and Vika hastened to her side with a trencher. "I pray for yer forgiveness. I did not want to take so long, but the serving maid…"

"Never mind," Adela admonished. "Just fill the chalice. Her mouth is dry."

"As you wish," Vika replied and handed a chalice to Adela.

"Take a sip, my darling. It will make you feel better."

Gavenia lifted her head and swilled the sweet mead, the honey-wine tingled her throat when she swallowed.

Her eyesight blurred a little, and she rested her head back on the pillows. "Mother, Vika. I want you both to take care of the babe. Help my child to remember its parents."

Adela's soft sobs were muffled by the hand over her mouth. Gavenia appreciated her mother's attempt at remaining strong.

"I will treat yer babe like it was my very own." Vika sat next to the bed, a reassuring smile across her face. "Here," she picked up the chalice, "take another sip."

CHAPTER SEVENTEEN

"Tell me where my father is, and I will grant you a hasty death," Callum said, his eyes glowing with vengeance.

Tremayne gritted his teeth and rose to his full height, hands clenched at his sides.

A grizzly soldier shouted, "His death should be slow and painful. Make him pay for yer father's capture."

A round of "ayes" came from several of the men who accompanied the young Roberts chieftain.

"I do not know where he is," Tremayne growled. He did not have time to converse. "Step aside, Roberts. I need a horse."

The soldiers laughed, and Callum smirked, "You are in naught position to be commanding."

Tremayne sighed. "By my troth, I did not know yer father was missing. I will help you find him later, but right now yer sister is in danger, she needs this potion."

"Think ye, I would let you poison my sister?"

"'Tis not a poison, and if you do not let me pass, I will break yer neck." Tremayne ignored the fact he was naked without weapons or powers, but he still had his hands and deadly determination.

The forest stillness was sliced with the roar of laughter.

Callum did not laugh, his eyes remained cold. "Lady Gavenia told me you saved her life and sacrificed yer own. Is that true?"

"I know it is hard for you to believe, but I love her," the unfamiliar words glided over his tongue. No words ever felt so right and true in the saying. "Please, we have wasted much time."

"Seamus," Callum called over his shoulder.

"Aye?" The youngest soldier straightened in the saddle.

"Give the Campbell yer mount."

Callum lowered his sword and his men grumbled, but silenced when their chieftain turned to glared at them. Undoing the blue cloak around his shoulders, Callum threw the warm garment at Tremayne.

"Cover yourself."

Tremayne nodded and limped over to the free horse. He suppressed the groan his body demanded when pulling himself into the saddle. He did not want these men to know how vulnerable he was in strength.

Callum sidled his steed close to Tremayne's horse. "If yer words prove false, I will cut off yer member and feed it to yer pack of wolves."

Tremayne nodded. "Agreed." He gathered the reins in his hand and looked at the horizon. The sun was setting in a ray of brilliant orange and red. This would be the last time he saw the sun.

He turned to Callum. "Try to keep up," he said, then sank his heels into the horse's flanks.

They rode through the eve to reach Gleich Castle. Less than a league away, Tremayne felt dizzy. His eyesight blurred while his stomach wanted to heave, but could not. Gavenia had been poisoned by his mother. The dire effects ravaged his system as it would through Gavenia. He cursed the horse for not going faster. Even if he had a fresh horse, he knew he would be too late to save her.

The mighty draw-gate from the castle appeared through the mist. Gleich Castle sat on the edge of a mountain, its stone walls surrounded the village and keep within.

Callum called to the gate keeper and the wooden gate slowly lowered.

"Come on, come on," Tremayne uttered. Even in its exhausted state, his mount side stepped nervously, no doubt feeling Tremayne's impatience.

Before the gate was flush on the ground, he turned his horse around and then galloped at the gate, urging his horse to leap into the air. They landed on the wooden plank and skidded down the rest of the way.

He galloped along the empty roads, the horse's hooves echoing through the sleepy village. Callum and his men had just passed over the gate. He could not wait for them.

Once at the castle, he threw himself off the horse and raced into the Great Hall. A tired sentry rubbed his eyes, disbelief on his face.

The guard went to stop him, but Tremayne punched him in the face, knocking him unconscious. He had no time to explain his presence. Pulling the cloak hood over his head, he undid the soldier's scabbard and wrapped it around his waist. He did not know where his mother was, but he wanted to be prepared.

The sleeping servants remained oblivious to him as he leaped over their bodies and ran up the stairs, two at a time. Gavenia's life-force was weak, but he could feel her fading energy on the second landing.

From down the hall, he heard someone crying from within a chamber, "I am so sorry, I am so sorry."

Tremayne's heart broke with the wretched sobs. Please, let her not be dead. He shoved the door open and charged into the chamber.

Drawing his sword, his gaze went to Gavenia. Her beautiful face lay peaceful, her arms crossed over her chest.

Nae! He was too late.

"She is dead," he accused and looked beyond Gavenia's mother to the lady standing in the corner, "and you killed her!"

Tremayne went to walk around the bed when Gavenia's mother blocked his path. "Who are you?"

Torella, in another lady's form, picked up the babe from the crib and held it against her chest.

Tremayne pushed Gavenia's mother to the side and held his sword at Torella's neck. "Give me the babe and I will spare yer life."

She smiled at him with self assurance. In a choked voice she cried, "Lady Adela, help me!"

"You know, Mother, if I kill you in another human's form, you will die for good."

Torella's eyes glowed red. Her mouth dropped into a frown. She whispered, "You will pay for betraying me."

A voice from behind started to chant. Dear Gods, Adela was cursing him. He must not take his gaze from Torella. "Give me the babe, now or die. I have nothing to lose!"

She handed over the baby. "One day, I will come for the child. And you will not be here to protect her." She disappeared into the wall.

His baby cooed in Tremayne's arms and he smiled down at the bundle. Suddenly, his chest began to ache, his heart slowed in beating. The sword dropped from his hand and he fell to his knees. Adela was killing him.

Adela grabbed the baby from his arms. "What did you do to Lady Vika?"

He clutched his chest, his heart being squeezed.

"That was my mother, not…not…Lady…Vi…"

"Mother!" Callum rushed into the room. "Release him."

"Why?"

"This is Laird Tremayne, he is here to save Gavenia." Callum rushed to his side.

Adela muttered a few words and his heart began to beat a normal rhythm.

"I do not understand any of this," Adela cried. "Callum, yer sister…"

Gavenia's brother kneeled at his sister's bedside. His head buried in Gavenia's hair.

"Wait," Tremayne breathed and struggled to his feet. "This might still work." He uncorked the vial and poured the contents through Gavenia's lips.

"Milady, Callum, I need you to hold hands and join a circle with Gavenia. Yer Celtic powers might be enough to save her."

"But she is dead," Callum roared.

"Only her body, her spirit is nearby. I can feel her." He looked at Gavenia's mother. "Trust me."

She nodded. Laying the babe on the pallet, she grabbed Callum's and Gavenia's hand. "What do we need to do?"

"Concentrate on yer love for her." After taking Callum's hand he then grasped Gavenia's chilled hand. He closed his eyes and breathed deeply. "Spirit of the underworld…'tis not her time…send her back to her body…this witch is mine."

Again and again, he chanted. But no movement came from the bed. A wave of apprehension swept through him. Damn his powers for not being with him.

"Tremayne?" Adela whispered his name.

He tilted his head up.

Tears marked Adela's cheeks. Her tone was resigned with sorrow, "My daughter loved you. I think she wanted you to know that."

Gavenia loved him? Nobody had ever loved him before.

He tightened his grip on the hands he held. Rising his voice, he chanted, "Spirit of the underworld…'tis not her time…send her back to her body…this witch is mine."

Gavenia did not move.

His body tensed, and he shouted, "Spirit of the underworld…'tis not her time…send her back to her body…this witch is mine!"

A cold breeze whooshed around the chamber, the candle scones flickered, half of them extinguished. The baby began to cry, and an eerie wail filled the room.

Tremayne held his eyes shut, unwilling to look down. He prayed that he did not fail her.

His hand was squeezed slightly, and he jumped at the touch. Glancing down, he witnessed the most beautiful thing on the earth—the deep blue of Gavenia's eyes.

Adela screamed for joy and Callum lifted his mother and swung her around.

Tremayne dropped to the side of the bed and gathered her into his arms. *Thank you, thank you, thank you...*

She smiled and it was the most perfect smile he had ever seen. Gavenia reached up and cupped his face with both hands. "Am I dead?"

Laughter bubbled up from his chest. "Nae, my love. You are alive."

Her gaze went from her brother standing at the end of the bed to her mother who sat down next to her. "Gavenia, you are well and alive."

A high pitch cry rented the air and Gavenia gasped. Was that her baby? The sorcerer rose, walked away and returned with a bundle in his arms.

"This is our baby," he said, his voice soft.

The Celtic Witch and the Sorcerer 151

She opened her arms and awkwardly gathered the infant. The little face was scrunched up, the babe's gums and tongue exposed as it cried. Her heart was filled with wonder and love as she cuddled the baby against her chest. With the sound of her heart beat, the newborn settled into a light slumber.

She looked up at her sorcerer garbed in a familiar blue cloak and a proud smile. Gavenia shook her head. "I canna believe you are here. I thought you were dead."

He looked out the window and then back to her. "Well, I will be soon." His tone was light, but Gavenia could see the under lying strain on his face.

"Is this the day of yer twenty-fifth birth?"

"Aye, and I know not my father's name."

Adela and Callum looked at each other, confused.

Gavenia explained, "If he does not find the name to his father before the sun rises, he will be cast into hell to atone for his mother's wickedness."

"That is awful!" Adela cried.

"Is there anything we can do?" Callum asked.

"Not unless you know the names of all the men Lady Torella slept with," Gavenia said, watching her sorcerer walk to the window.

"The sky brightens; soon the rays will break through." He returned to the bedside and leaned over to kiss her.

She could not lose him again. Not like this.

"Wait!" Adela leaped from the bed. "I remember a friend of yer father's was in love with Lady Torella. Perhaps he could be...Aye! The time fits. 'Twas over twenty-five winters ago when they were together."

"My mother had many lovers."

"Aye, but 'tis worth a try," Adela reasoned.

"Please, Tremayne, give the name a try," Gavenia pleaded.

Tremayne looked at the mother of his child, her pretty blue eyes full of sorrow. "That is the first time you have said my name." He kissed her lightly on the lips and nodded. "I will start the ritual."

The sword lay abandoned on the floor beneath the window and he picked it up. Outside, the sky turned pink. The sun was about to rise. He did not have much time left to complete the ritual. Hopefully, he would correctly remember the words from the ancient book of Dark Magick. One mislaid word, and the ritual would fail.

Using the sharp edge of the sword, he sliced his hand. Blood dripped over the blade toward the tip. He faced east, and then ran the sword's tip along the stones in a circle.

He turned to Adela. "What be my father's name?"

She stepped close and whispered into his ear.

Tremayne sighed and nodded. After so long searching, he finally knew his father's name.

He trained his gaze on Gavenia. She had risen from the bed. Standing on the outside of the circle in a white linen chemise, she lovingly held their babe in her arms. She was so beautiful.

He stepped into the circle. In a loud voice, he began the ritual, "Be this the day of my birth. I, Laird Tremayne Campbell offer my blood as a blessing to the Gods. I pray you redeem my sorcerer's heritage with my mortal father's ancestry. In the name of Master Dougal MacEwen, I seek redemption."

The sun was yet to peek over the horizon.

"Did it work?" Gavenia asked.

His body felt the same way.

"I think not." He committed her beauty to his memory. "Gavenia, I do not have much time." He swallowed the lump in his throat and held out his hand. "I love you."

Gavenia's lips tightened and she gave the babe to her mother. She picked up the sword. Slicing her hand, she stepped into the circle and roughly grasped his bloody hand, mingling their blood. She pressed her body against his.

"Hear me now, oh great Gods. I am Lady Gavenia Roberts…Celtic Witch. I share my enchanted blood with his." Her gaze was determined, her voice, strong. "I am his and he is mine. I will *not* release his soul!"

A thunder clap boomed outside and a gusty wind blew through the chamber, knocking the tapestry off the wall and breaking a chalice, but Tremayne and Gavenia held tightly to one another. Their eyes locked in each others' gaze. A green light surrounded them in a cocoon and lifted them from the floor.

Gavenia's mother shouted something, but Tremayne could barely hear over the noise of the wind. He put his arms around Gavenia and held her close. This was what it felt like to be loved. If he was going to hell, at least he did so with her words in his heart.

The green light disappeared and they fell to the floor.

He pushed himself up and crawled over to where Gavenia lay sprawled. "Are you all right?"

Gavenia allowed Tremayne to help her to her feet. She looked up and gasped. Sun rays shined on his handsome face.

"Tremayne, you are still here."

He stared over her shoulder, out the window. A smile stretched across his face. He lowered his head and lovingly kissed her. Her heart swelled with happiness.

"Hazzah!" Callum shouted from behind and they turned to laugh.

Her mother smiled, swaying the babe in her arms. "It gladdens my heart to see all is well." A wail came from the bundle in her arms. "I think this little one needs a feed."

Gavenia held onto Tremayne's hand and led him over to the bed, where she propped up her back with pillows.

Adela lowered her baby into her arms, and Gavenia shifted the gown to the side, allowing access to one of her breasts.

Tremayne lay on the bed and watched with fascination.

Callum and her mother excused themselves and went to leave.

"Where is my milady wife?" Callum asked her mother.

Adela sighed and placed her arm around his shoulders. "About yer wife…"

The door closed behind them, leaving the chamber in silence with the exception of sucking noises coming from their baby.

Gavenia smiled down at their child. She unwrapped the cloth around her baby to find the gender. She was so happy. Gavenia smiled at her sorcerer. Her love.

"Pray tell me, is she a lass?" Tremayne's voice was light.

"Aye, we have a Celtic witch."

"A Celtic witch and a sorceress," he corrected and kissed his daughter's plump hand.

"May the Gods help us all."

"We do not need their help." Tremayne shuffled closer to her and kissed her on the lips. "We have each other."

THE END

Read on for a sneak preview of **Heart of a Warlock**, *book three in Lyn Armstrong's Celtic Witch Series.*

Available July, 2008
Resplendence Publishing
www.ResplendencePublishing.com

CHAPTER ONE

Darkness.

Alayne Duncan would be forever cursed to live in darkness. No matter how much she blinked or rubbed her eyes, her sight would not return. She would never see another sunrise or the deep ruby color of a rose in full bloom. Nae, she would only see vague shadows and outlines.

What had she done?

This could have been avoided. She could have had her sight back if only she obeyed Lady Torella. The wicked sorceress gave her one opportunity to regain her sight. All she had to do was keep Laird Tremayne, the sorceress' son, imprisoned within the enchanted house.

But she could not do it.

His lady love was going to be killed if Alayne did not help him escape.

But where did that decision leave her now? It left her blind…forever.

Alayne rose from the kitchen table, the same place she had been sitting since Tremayne had left. She hoped he was not too late to save his lady. Or else her sacrifice would have been for naught.

Instead of thinking of his fate, she should be more concerned with her own future. Now that she thwarted

Torella's plans, it was only a matter of time before the sorceress returned to punish her.

Fear sliced through Alayne's heart like an icy dagger.

She had to leave!

Pivoting, she hastened toward the kitchen wall, her hand outstretched to feel the rough texture of the timber boards. She guided herself toward the stairway. The cool banister led up to the second landing where she shuffled along to the end chamber.

Thump.

"Ouch!"

Alayne hopped on one foot while grabbing her throbbing toe. The floorboards creaked under her weight as she limped to the bed. Being blind was the hardest thing she ever had to endure.

Nae, that was not true. Being parted from her younger sister, Wynda, was far worse. Although Alayne's wealth and titles were stripped from her by the King, it had been harder to watch her sister struggle against the soldiers as they escorted her out of the Great Hall before judgment was passed on Alayne. Wynda's screams remained fresh in her memory.

Forced to leave her home with nothing but the clothes she wore, Alayne had wandered alone through the woods. She had no where to go and nobody to help her. That was when she met the sorceress.

Taking a deep breath, she willed herself not think of the past. She had more pressing matters to worry about. Her life depended on her leaving immediately.

Edging along the pallet, Alayne used her tender toes to nudge the hard wooden chest at the end of the bed. Lifting the lid, she felt a cloth sack beneath her linen gowns and began to shove her clothes into the satchel.

A trickle of sweat made a trail along her temples. Where was she going to go? She had no place to seek refuge.

Perhaps a tavern would be in need of a laundress.
A blind laundress?

"Curse my fortune!" The words echoed in the empty chamber.

She rose with the sack and slung it over her shoulder. She must make haste before the sorceress returned for vengeance.

Alayne ran her hand down the balustrade, the steps creaking beneath her. She rushed into the kitchen to open a cupboard in the corner. The crash of clay pots landed near her feet as she swept them off the shelf. The smell of flour rose around her, and she felt the sprinkling of light dust settle on her skin.

"It must be here somewhere."

Her fingers grazed along a smooth barrel-shaped container.

Dropping her sack, she grasped the container and opened the lid. Inside rattled three gold coins. She tipped them into her hands and pocketed the only wealth she possessed. Picking up her belongings, Alayne felt along the wall for the place where she left her slippers. Bending down, she placed the shoes on her feet and then opened the back door.

"Where am I to go?" she asked herself again.

Being exiled from her lands, she was unable to return to the Duncan Clan. The unforgivable crimes they accused her of were something she could not face. Not now. Not with her blindness.

Alayne took a deep breath and raised her chin. One day she would clear her name and they could once again be a family. For now, she had to survive, for her sister's sake.

The oak door creaked as she closed it behind her.

"I do not know where I am bound for, but I cannot stay here."

She moved toward the smell of sweet hay. One, two, three steps to the right and she was at the entrance of the small barn. She groped for the handle and pulled the doors open. Her palfrey gave a long, high pitched sound in welcome. Alayne smiled with relief.

Following the sound of the neigh, she reached out. A silky nose nuzzled her palm. Running her hand along the warm pelt, she grabbed a handful of mane and swung up onto the horse's bare back.

"Make haste, my friend."

Alayne gently heeled the flanks and balanced her sack on her lap as the horse's steady gait led them outside. "We must away before…"

A sense of stillness surrounded her as if the very air weighed heavy with evil. Fear rose in her throat, her tongue tasted of bile.

The sorceress!

It was too late.

Her horse sidestepped with nervousness and then reared. Alayne was unbalanced and fell off. Her backside landed in mud, its gooey mass oozing between her fingers. After a sharp stench reached her nose, she knew it was not mud, but…

"Shit!"

Of all the places she could have landed.

A shrill cackle rented the air.

Alayne froze.

Her breath seemed to harden in her throat. All she could see was darkness. Forever, darkness!

She jolted when a whisper tickled her ear, "Did the wee lass think she could escape my wrath?"

Alayne's heart dropped, her stomach twisting into a knot.

Slowly, she shook her head and lowered her chin.

Sharp nails dug into her arm through the thin fabric of her simple gown, pulling her to her feet. Despair spread throughout Alayne, causing her limbs to weaken, threatening her legs to collapse.

Silently, Alayne prayed that death would come swiftly.

* * * * *

"Where is the sorceress?" Laird Callum, Chieftain of the Roberts Clan, demanded of the prisoner chained to the wall. Sweat moistened his brow, but he would not release the whip in his hand. He would find the devil's mistress, even if he had to kill the man before him.

The sharp crack echoed throughout the dungeon as Callum slashed the whip across the prisoner's bare back. "Where is she?"

The Campbell's wiry old steward remained silent, frustrating Callum. He took no pleasure in torture, but he would do what was necessary to find the sorceress, the only person who knew where his father was being held.

"We have been over this many times. You know where she is, you have served the dark mistress all your life. Tell me and I will release you."

The steward twisted around to glare at Callum. "Why do you not ask Laird Tremayne?" he sneered. "Or does he keep his mother's whereabouts a secret from his new clan?"

Callum pulled the steward's damp brown hair, tilting his head back. "You are the one who is the traitor, Master Evan. You tried to kill my sister, your laird's wife."

"She was not his wife when I stabbed her and besides, she is well and hearty, perhaps that should account for something."

"*That* is the only reason you still live," Callum growled and released his hold. "Maychance, another day without food and water will release your tongue."

The sound of laughter followed Callum up the stairwell, even after the heavy dungeon door closed behind him. The steward flamed the suspicions in the back of his mind about his sister's husband. Did the sorcerer not have the same wicked blood in his veins as his mother? Laird Tremayne *had* imprisoned his sister to use her magical Celtic blood to resurrect his mother from purgatory.

And now he was married into the Roberts clan. Campbells and Roberts. Two feuding clans. He could not believe it. If his missing father only knew the pledge he made to his grandfather had come to fruition.

No matter how much Callum disagreed with the alliance, his hatred focused on another Campbell. Lady Torella, the sorceress who stole the life of his betrothed and imprisoned his father. It had been a full year and still he could not find either of them. He did not even know if his father was still alive.

If anything happened to him, Callum swore he would have vengeance.

His boots rang as he stormed into the solar. The warm chamber was deserted.

Where was everyone?

A gurgling sound came from a wooden box near the window. Callum hastened toward the squeal and found his bonny niece kicking her legs playfully. Upon seeing him, baby Rhiannon giggled and threw her pudgy hands toward him.

Callum's anger melted and he gathered her into his arms. Her soft white gown flowed over her legs as he lifted her up into the air.

He cooed, "Who left you all alone?" Even though his voice was soft, the question was one that vexed him.

Rhiannon was never to be left alone. It was not safe. Even with a family of witches, he feared the sorceress was more powerful. Rhiannon had the blood of a sorceress and a Celtic witch. A mixture of good and evil. Whoever had the babe, had supreme magick. A temptation Lady Torella would not walk away from lightly. The sorceress would come for Rhiannon. It was only a matter of time.

"Ah, there you are."

At the sound of his mother's lilting voice, Callum gathered Rhiannon to his chest and turned.

"Where is the wet nurse?" he asked, keeping his tone light so as not to frighten his niece.

Adela glided into the room and forced a smile while caressing Rhiannon's pink cheek with the back of her finger. "I sent her on an errand."

"Mother, Rhiannon is never to be left unguarded. The sorceress could have…"

"I did not leave her for long and I would sense if the sorceress was nearby."

The baby in his arms began to get restless, so he swayed her as he had seen his sister do many times. "You did not sense the sorceress when she was masquerading as my betrothed."

His mother's beautiful face fell and Callum instantly regretted the accusation.

"Your father's absence had taken a toll on me."

"I pray your pardon, Mother, I…"

Adela placed her arm around his waist and he pulled her into his embrace. "There is nothing to pardon, my son. But I swear to you, I will never let my guard down again," she said as her gaze, affectionate once more, touched Rhiannon.

Sniffing the air, his mother informed, "I think the wee lass needs to be changed." Taking the babe, she returned her to the box. "Your sister and Tremayne should be returning shortly."

"Where did they go?"

"Your sister convinced Tremayne to take her for a ride to the lake. You know how she gets when she is cooped up inside all day long."

"Aye, I do."

"I insisted they leave Rhiannon here with me to give them a respite." Adela folded a fresh cloth around the baby and picked her up again. His mother looked at him with a serious gaze. "Tremayne talks of his home again."

"Well, he can talk all he likes. They are not leaving until I find Father," Callum growled and stormed to the sideboard. Picking up a trencher, he placed an assortment of victuals inside.

"You do not trust your new brother?" Adela asked, her brow furrowed.

"Nae, I do not. He is his mother's son after all. No matter how much he despises the sorceress, he is still connected to her."

"He is also your sister's *chosen one* and will not hurt her or the babe."

"Chosen one," he scoffed. "Where was his loyalty when he held my sister against her will or tried to kill her for the sake of his mother?"

"But he did not. He risked his life for Gavenia."

"I care not. I do not trust him and he will remain our *guest* until I can be assured of Gavenia's and Rhiannon's safety."

"Wield your sword lightly, my son. You do not want to alienate your sister."

Callum turned his back on his mother. "I am Chieftain of the Roberts clan. Until I find my father and avenge my betrothed, no one is leaving."

His mother touched his shoulder and gently turned him to face her. "You look just like your father. You have the same golden hair and strong jaw line. But your angelic features belie the Roberts stubborn streak." She touched his face, her voice softened, "Do not let vengeance darken your heart, my son."

"Right now, my heart is cold. And 'tis the way I like it." He dropped the trencher on the sideboard and turned to his mother. "If anyone is helping the sorceress, be it Laird Tremayne or someone else...I pledge to you, I will see them dead!"

ABOUT THE AUTHOR

Photograph by Rod Vella. www.RStudios.com.au

Born in Queensland, Australia, Lyn Armstrong has a passion for writing historical romance with an erotic element. This self-confessed romantic wrote her first novel in the early 1990's and has been writing ever since. Along with touring the countries she writes about, Lyn has served on the board of Florida Romance Writers. When she is not lost in the mystical world of Scottish lairds and enticing witches, she enjoys spending time with family and friends.

Also available from Resplendence Publishing:

The Last Celtic Witch by Lyn Armstrong:

"As charming and magical as Celtic legend itself, a truly enjoyable read and wonderful debut!"

Heather Graham
New York Times Bestselling Author

A painful death... a prophecy foretold.

Pursued by evil forces for her powers, recluse Adela MacAye foresees her own agonizing death. She must seek the chosen one to produce an heir and pass on her Celtic powers. To fail would be the end of good magick, plunging the world into darkness.

Conjuring a fertility spell she is led to a sensual chieftain who is betrothed to the sorceress that hunts her. Time is running out as fate and the future pursue her.

Plagued by enemies and undermined by sabotage, handsome Laird Phillip Roberts must save his clan from bloody feud by making an alliance through marriage... a marriage he does not want. After a night of white-hot sensual delights with the alluring witch, his heart commands he break the pledge of peace. With treachery around every corner, will he be too late to save... The Last Celtic Witch?

$4.50 e-book, $12.99 print

The Curse: Book One in the Legend of Blackbeard's Chalice by Maddie James.

"I felt as if I lived every thrilling moment of THE CURSE. Maddie James writes pulse-pounding suspense and riveting romance!"

Teresa Medeiros
New York Times Bestselling Author

Jack Porter is in hot pursuit of his kidnapped wife. Not an easy feat considering it is 1718 and the kidnapper is the notorious pirate, Edward Teach aka. Blackbeard. Determined to rescue his wife, Hannah, and take the pirate's head in the process, Jack sneaks aboard the pirate's ship but is too late. Hannah dies in his arms.

Nearly 300 years later, Claire Winslow vacations on a secluded east coast island, where the image of a man walking the misty shore haunts her. Then he comes to her one night, kisses her, and disappears. The next night they make love and he tells her his name is Jack. But did they really make love? Or was it a dream? And why did he call her Hannah?

The Curse sends Jack and Claire on a wild search through time for a powerful historical artifact – the silver-plated chalice made from Blackbeard's skull. This chalice holds the key to their destiny and their love. Only with the chalice will they be able to reverse Blackbeard's Curse.

Will they find it in time? Or are they destined to be parted by fate once more?

$6.50 e-book, $19.99 print

Rules of Darkness by Tia Fanning

One special gift...Twelve rules to follow...There are some rules that should never be broken.

They tell me that I am special, that my ability to heal mental illness is a "gift" that should be treasured and appreciated. As far as I'm concerned, I'm not gifted...I'm cursed. Nothing in this life is free, not even gifts. There is always a price to be paid somewhere, somehow.

My healing gift came with twelve Rules of Darkness, rules that I must follow at all times, until the day I die. The rules are ingrained in who I am. They dictate how I live my life when I am awake, and they haunt me when I'm asleep. *Don't look into a graveyard, Katia. Don't touch the dead, Katia. Never seek out the lost, Katia...*It's enough to drive a person mad.

And perhaps that's where I find myself now. A victim of a disease I can cure in others, but not in myself. It's madness to break the rules, and yet, I don't care anymore. I'm tired of living my life this way. I'm tired of the rules. I won't do it any more, and if that means I suffer the consequences, then so be it.

$4.50 e-book, $11.99 print

Find Resplendence Titles at the following retailers:

Resplendence Publishing:

www.resplendencepublishing.com

Amazon.com:

www.amazon.com

Target.com:

www.target.com

Fictionwise:

www.fictionwise.com

Mobipocket:

www.mobipocket.com

1328931

Made in the USA